STRANGER THINGS

ERICA THE GREAT

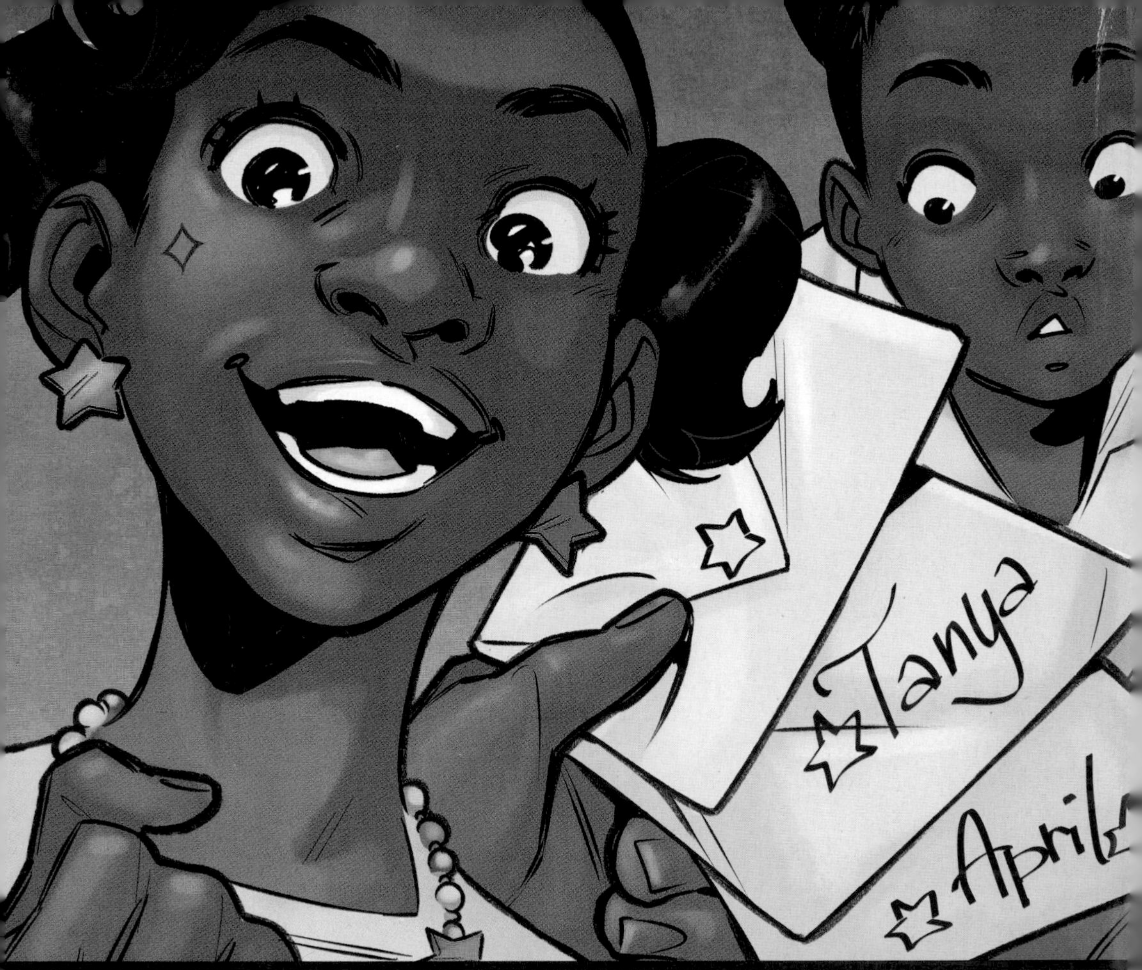

Tanya
April

STRANGER THINGS

ERICA THE GREAT

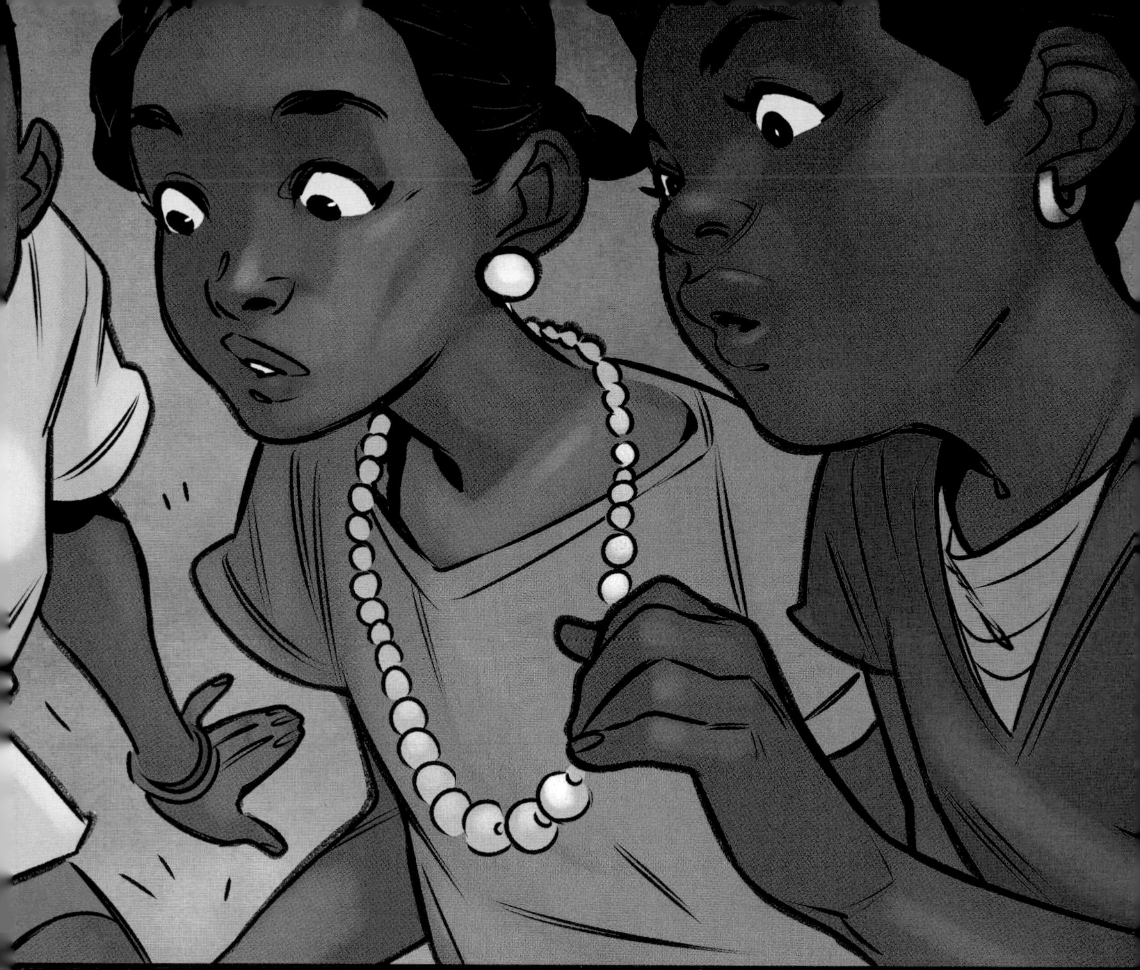

Script by
DANNY LORE and **GREG PAK**

Art by
VALERIA FAVOCCIA

Colors by
DAN JACKSON

Lettering by
NATE PIEKOS of **BLAMBOT®**

Cover Art by
RON CHAN

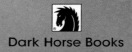

Dark Horse Books

President & Publisher
MIKE RICHARDSON

Editor
SPENCER CUSHING

Assistant Editor
KONNER KNUDSEN

Designer
PATRICK SATTERFIELD

Digital Art Technician
ALLYSON HALLER

Special thanks to Joe Lawson and Cindy Chang of Netflix.

Published by DARK HORSE BOOKS
A division of Dark Horse Comics LLC.
10956 SE Main Street
Milwaukie, OR 97222

DarkHorse.com | Netflix.com

First edition: January 2022
eBook ISBN 978-1-50671-504-9
ISBN 978-1-50671-454-7

10 9 8 7 6 5 4 3 2 1
Printed in China

To find a comics shop in your area, visit comicshoplocator.com

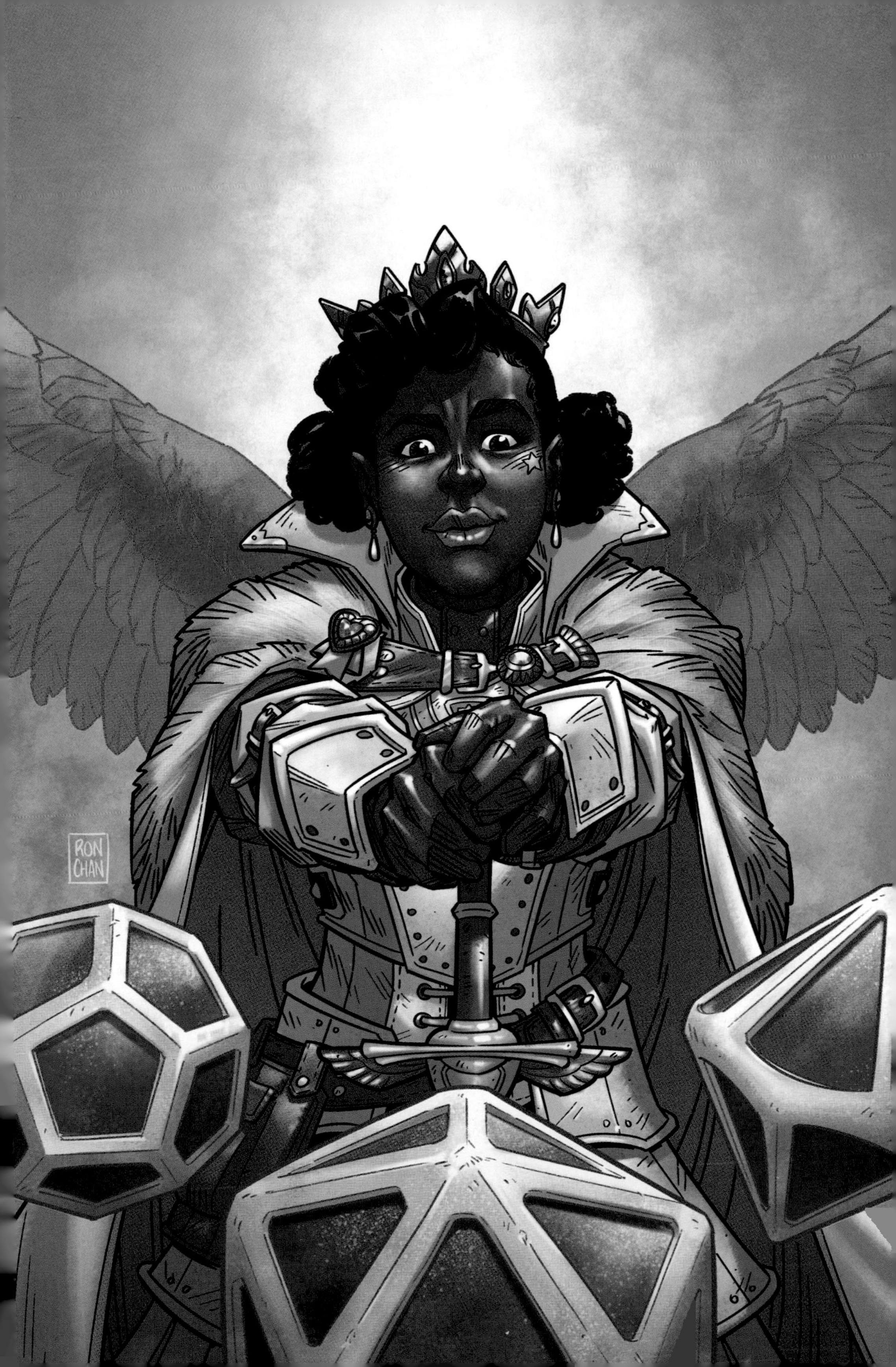
RON
CHAN

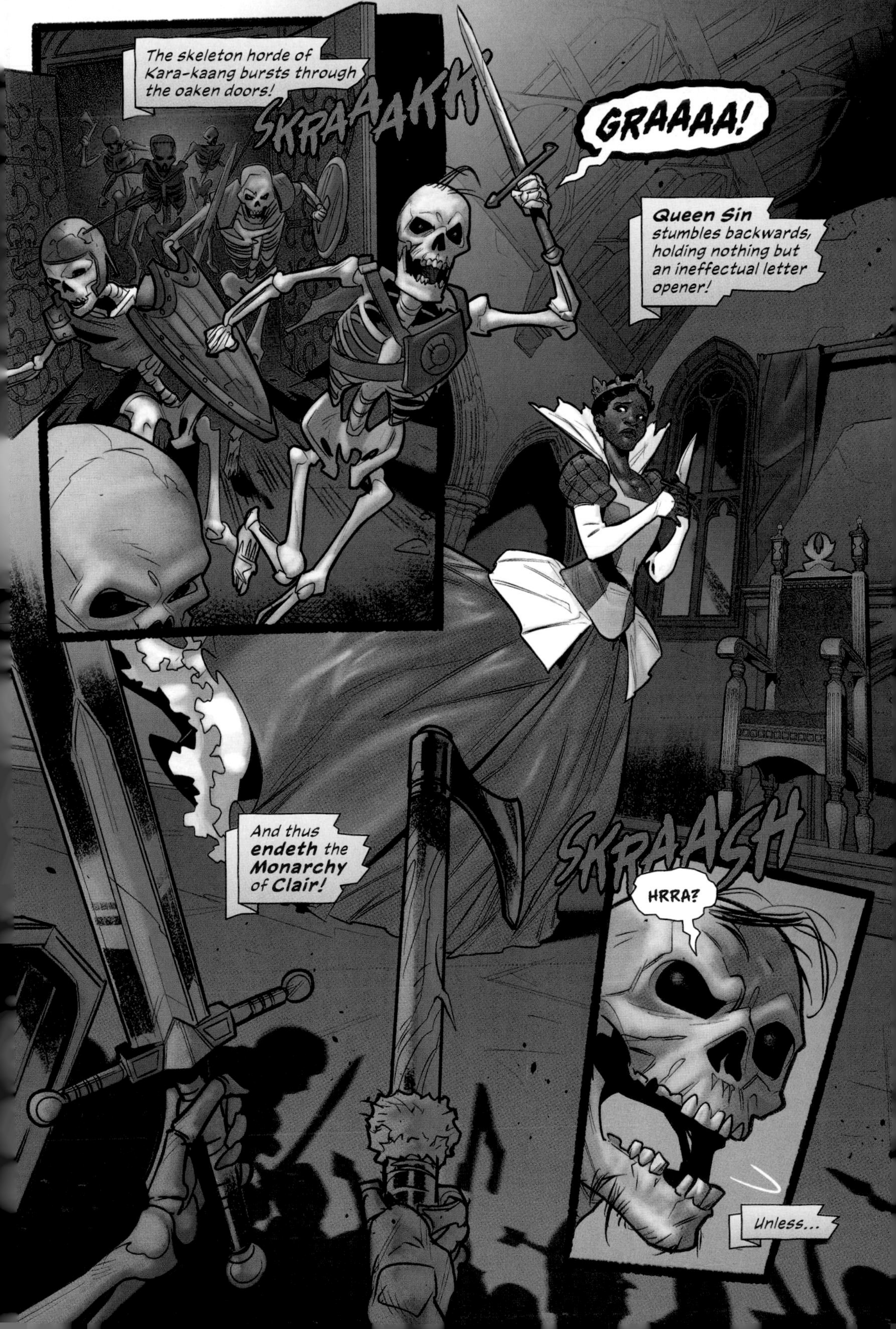
The skeleton horde of Kara-kaang bursts through the oaken doors!
SKRAAAKK
GRAAAA!
Queen Sin stumbles backwards, holding nothing but an ineffectual letter opener!
And thus endeth the Monarchy of Clair!
SKRAASH
HRRA?
Unless...

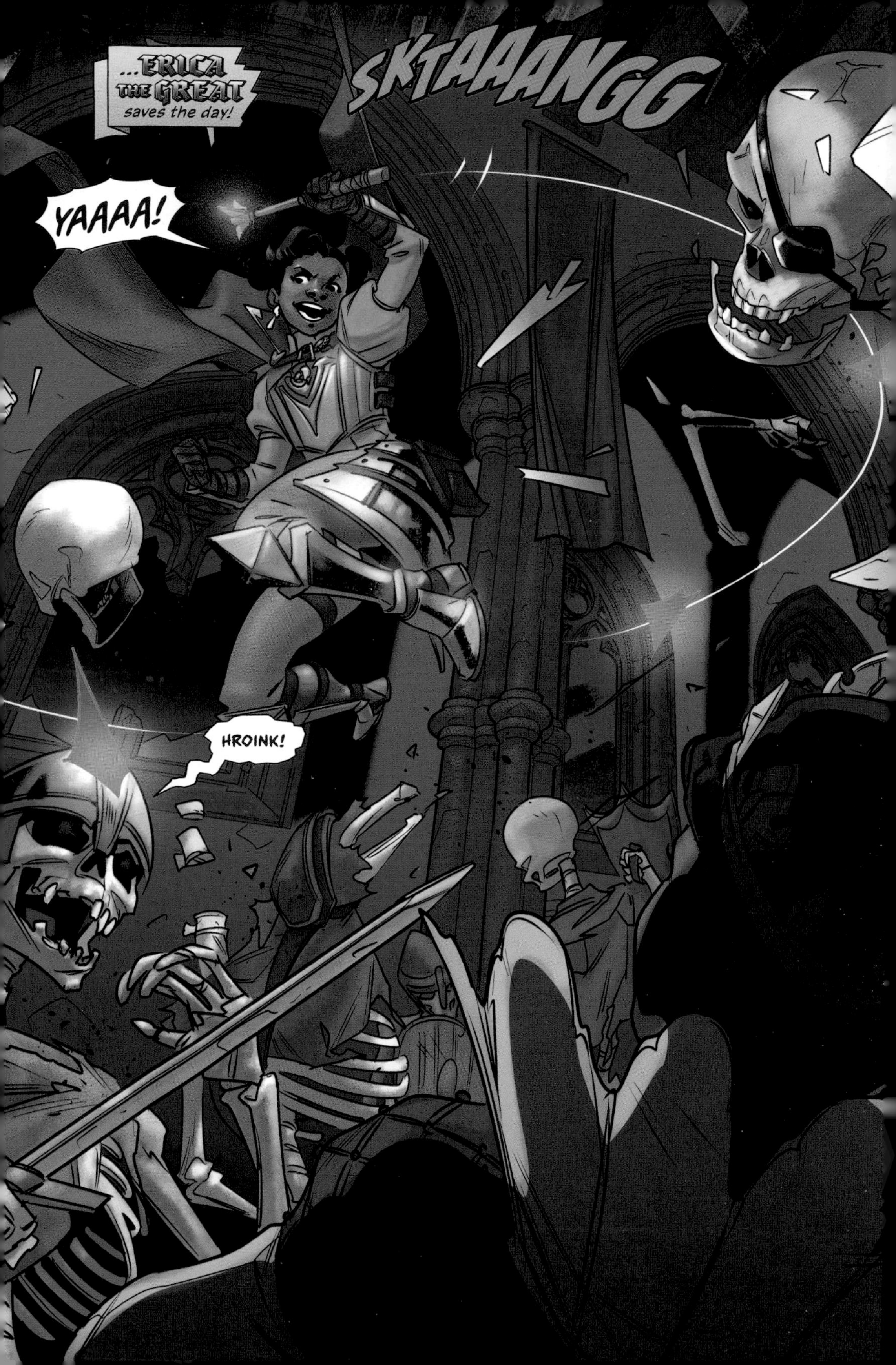
...ERICA THE GREAT saves the day!
SKTAAANGG
YAAAA!
HROINK!

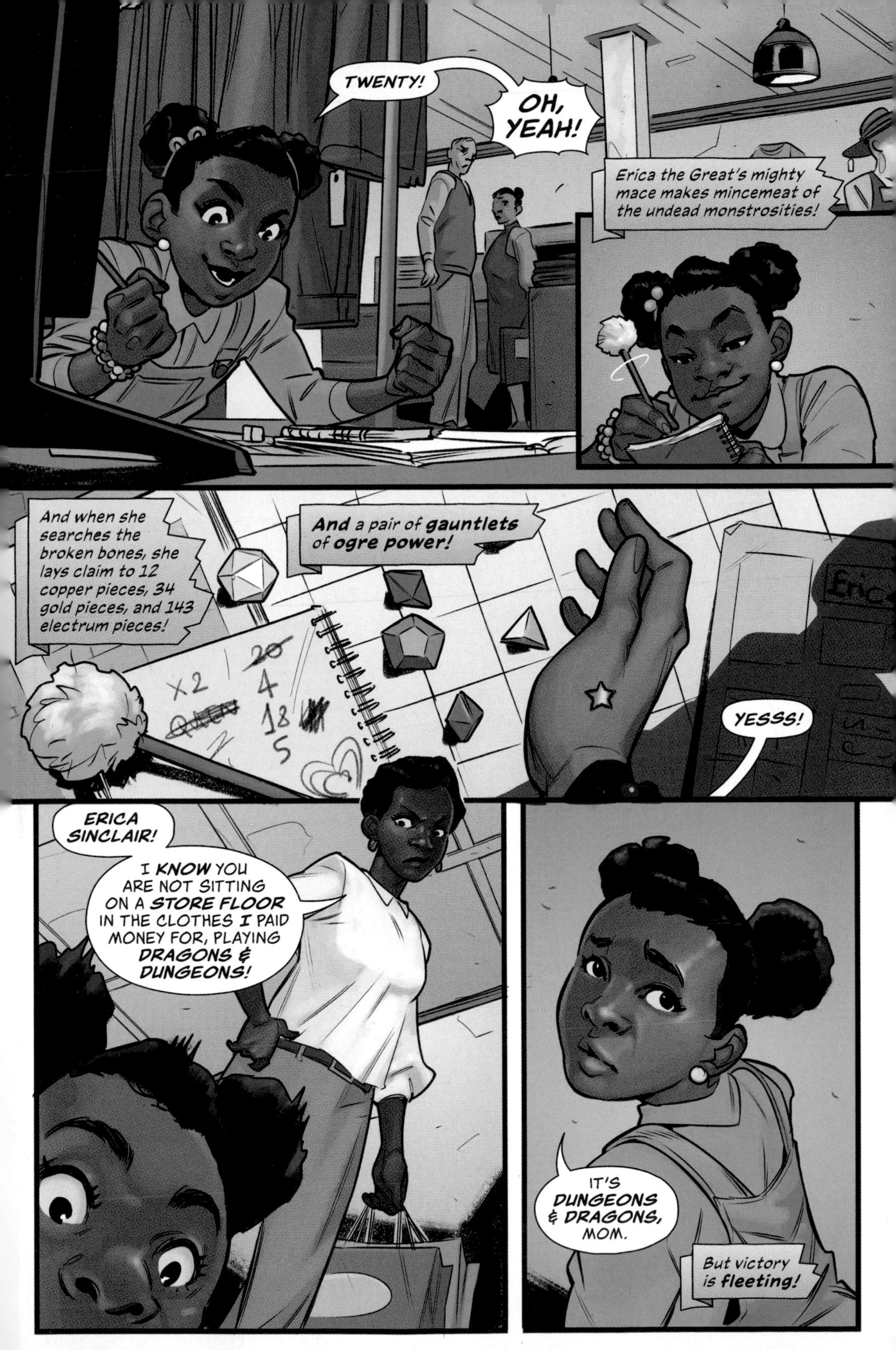

TWENTY!
OH, YEAH!
Erica the Great's mighty mace makes mincemeat of the undead monstrosities!
And when she searches the broken bones, she lays claim to 12 copper pieces, 34 gold pieces, and 143 electrum pieces!
And a pair of gauntlets of ogre power!
YESSS!
ERICA SINCLAIR!
I KNOW YOU ARE NOT SITTING ON A STORE FLOOR IN THE CLOTHES I PAID MONEY FOR, PLAYING DRAGONS & DUNGEONS!
IT'S DUNGEONS & DRAGONS, MOM.
But victory is fleeting!

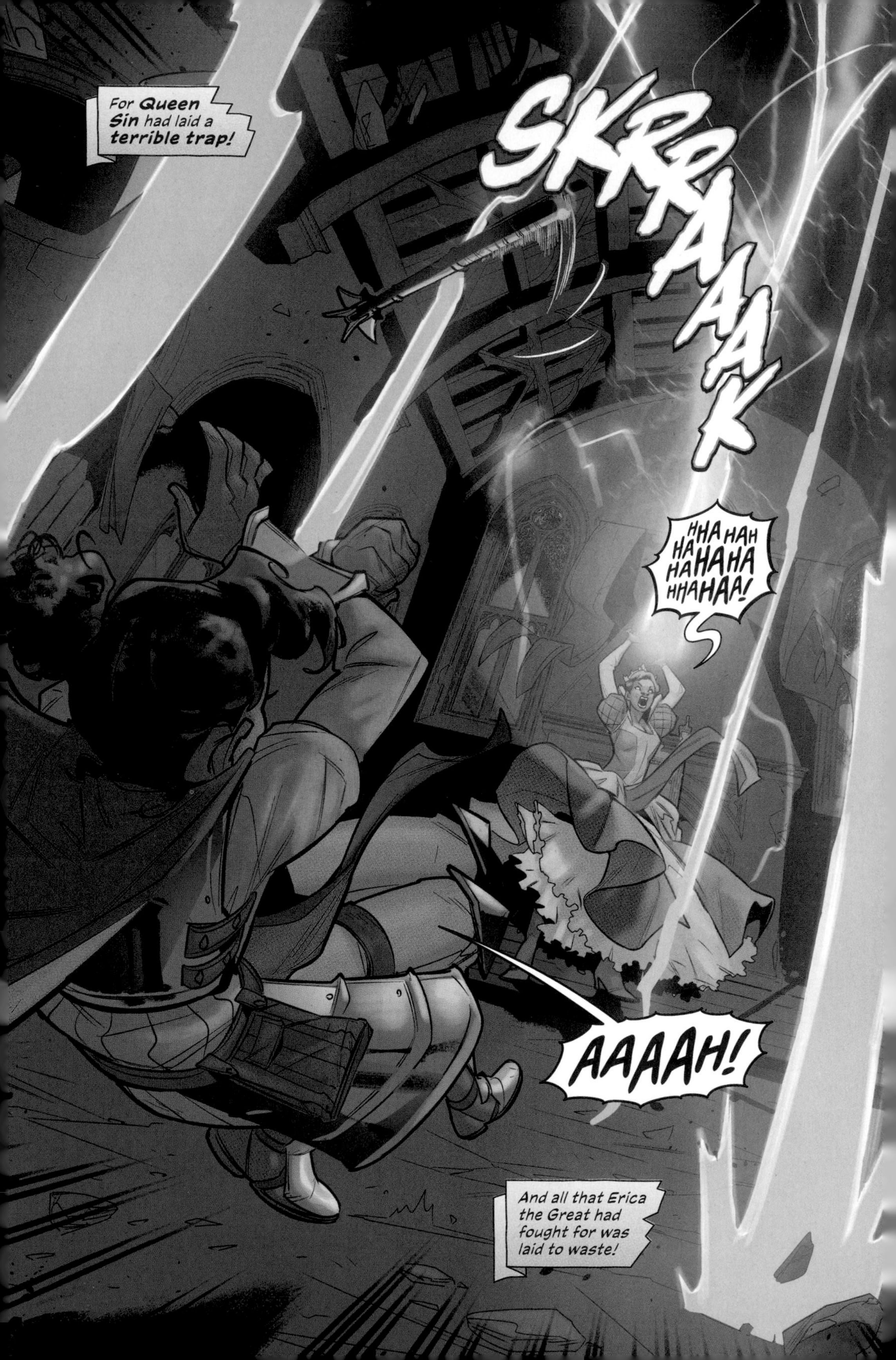
For Queen Sin had laid a terrible trap!
SKRRAAAAK
HHA HAH HA HAHAHA HAHAHA HHAHAA!
AAAAH!
And all that Erica the Great had fought for was laid to waste!

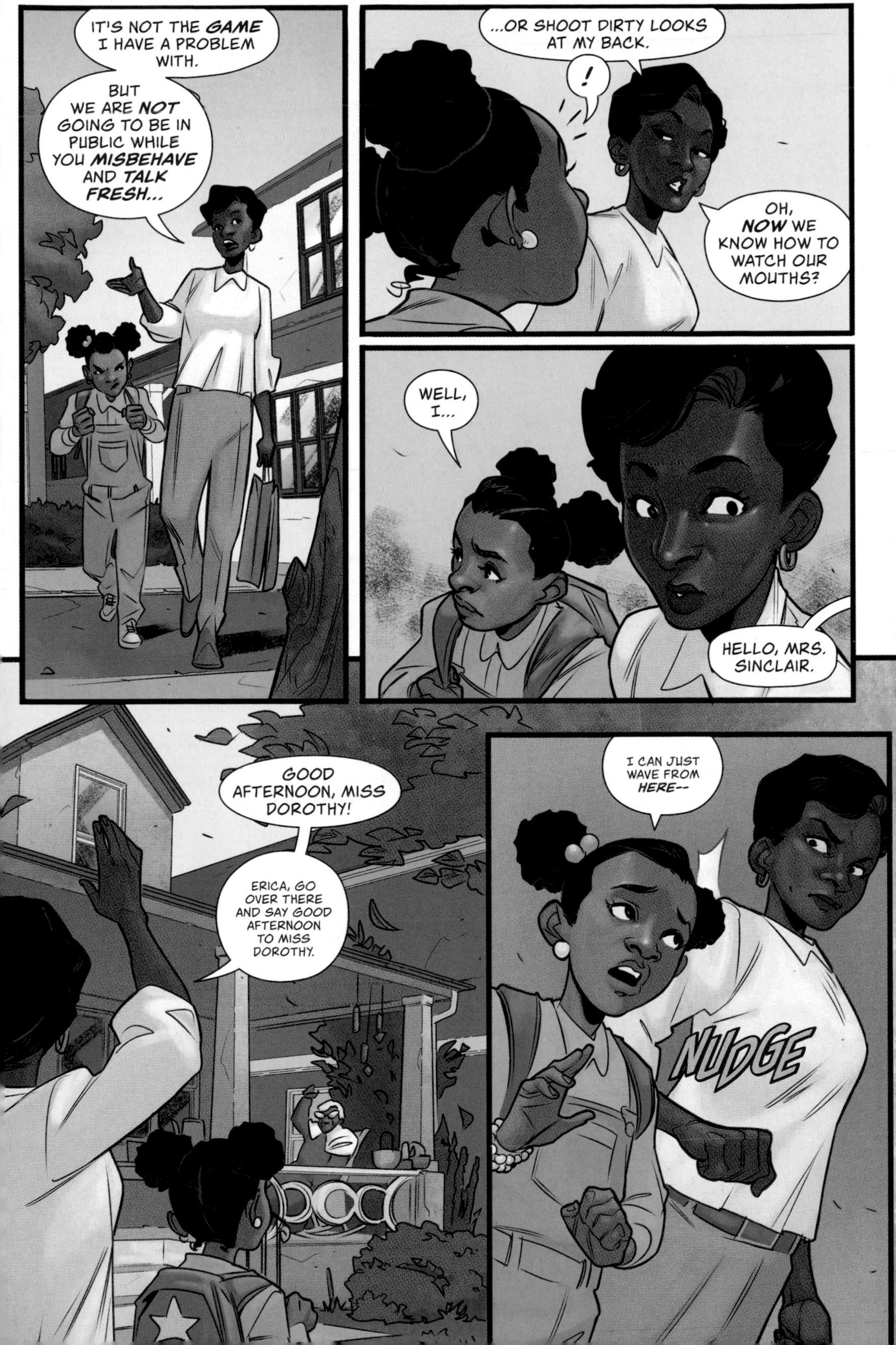
IT'S NOT THE GAME I HAVE A PROBLEM WITH.
BUT WE ARE NOT GOING TO BE IN PUBLIC WHILE YOU MISBEHAVE AND TALK FRESH...
...OR SHOOT DIRTY LOOKS AT MY BACK.
!
OH, NOW WE KNOW HOW TO WATCH OUR MOUTHS?
WELL, I...
HELLO, MRS. SINCLAIR.
GOOD AFTERNOON, MISS DOROTHY!
ERICA, GO OVER THERE AND SAY GOOD AFTERNOON TO MISS DOROTHY.
I CAN JUST WAVE FROM HERE--
NUDGE

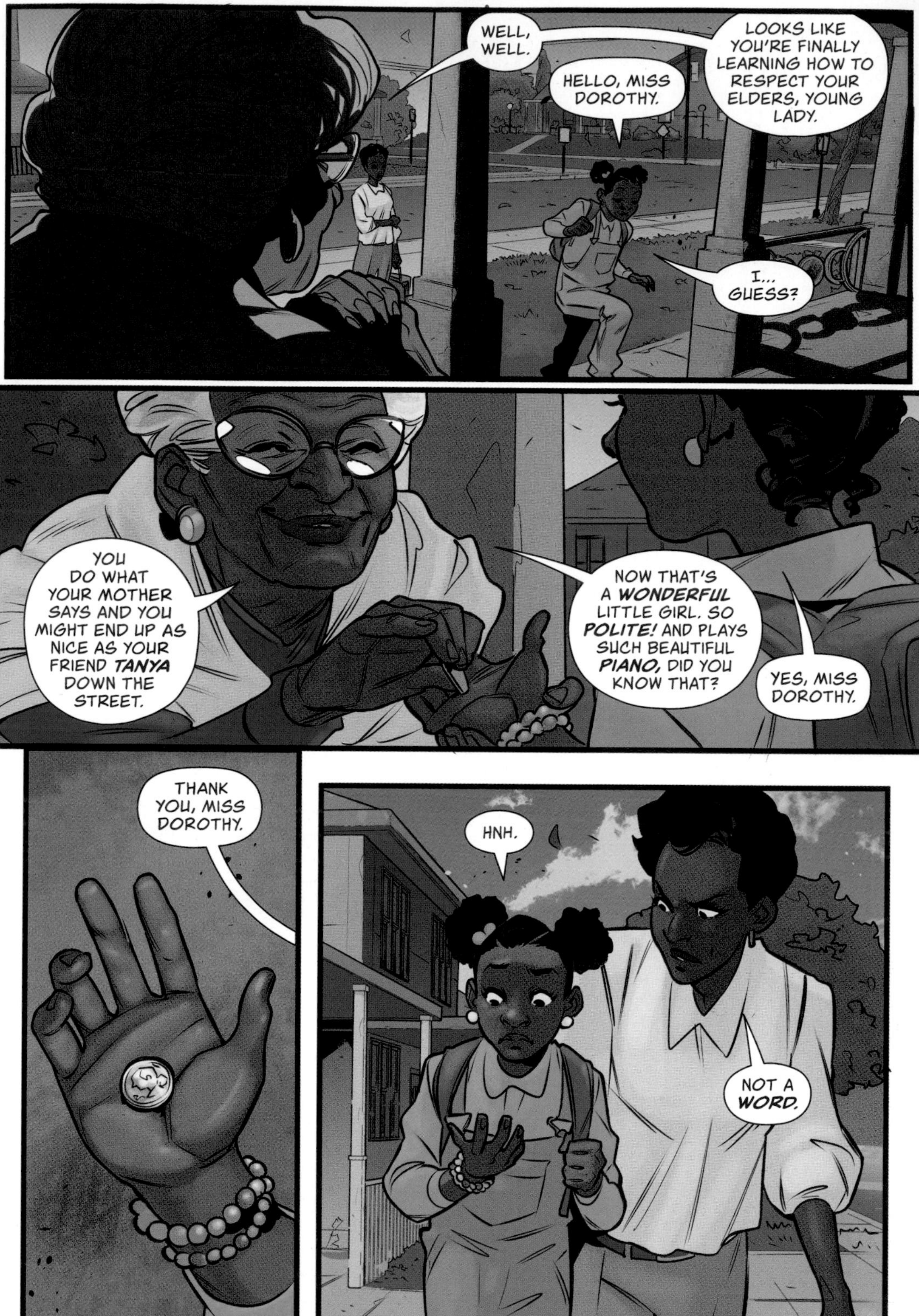
WELL, WELL.
HELLO, MISS DOROTHY.
LOOKS LIKE YOU'RE FINALLY LEARNING HOW TO RESPECT YOUR ELDERS, YOUNG LADY.
I... GUESS?
YOU DO WHAT YOUR MOTHER SAYS AND YOU MIGHT END UP AS NICE AS YOUR FRIEND TANYA DOWN THE STREET.
NOW THAT'S A WONDERFUL LITTLE GIRL. SO POLITE! AND PLAYS SUCH BEAUTIFUL PIANO, DID YOU KNOW THAT?
YES, MISS DOROTHY.
THANK YOU, MISS DOROTHY.
HNH.
NOT A WORD.

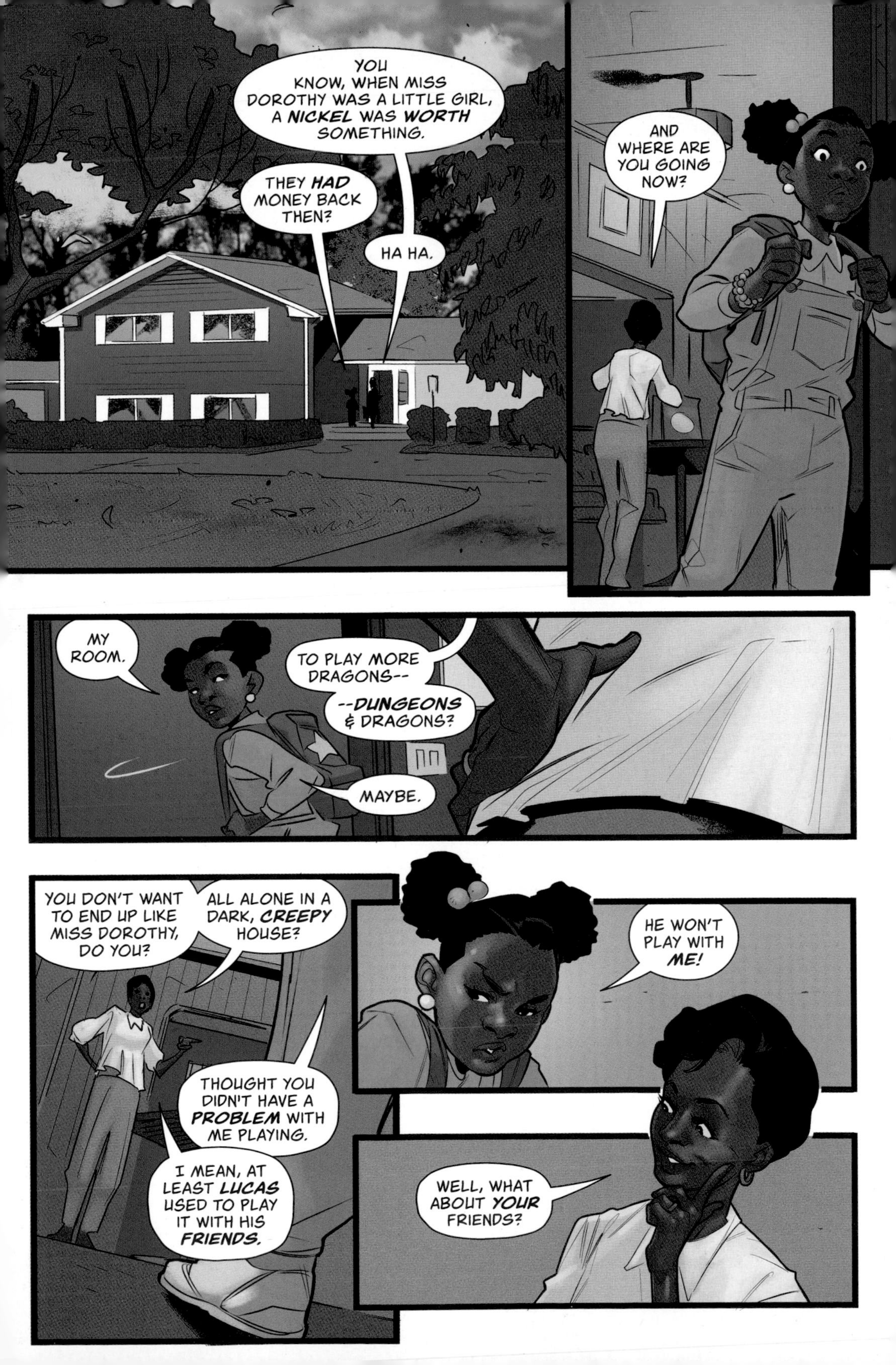
YOU KNOW, WHEN MISS DOROTHY WAS A LITTLE GIRL, A NICKEL WAS WORTH SOMETHING.
THEY HAD MONEY BACK THEN?
HA HA.
AND WHERE ARE YOU GOING NOW?
MY ROOM.
TO PLAY MORE DRAGONS--
--DUNGEONS & DRAGONS?
MAYBE.
YOU DON'T WANT TO END UP LIKE MISS DOROTHY, DO YOU?
ALL ALONE IN A DARK, CREEPY HOUSE?
THOUGHT YOU DIDN'T HAVE A PROBLEM WITH ME PLAYING.
I MEAN, AT LEAST LUCAS USED TO PLAY IT WITH HIS FRIENDS.
HE WON'T PLAY WITH ME!
WELL, WHAT ABOUT YOUR FRIENDS?

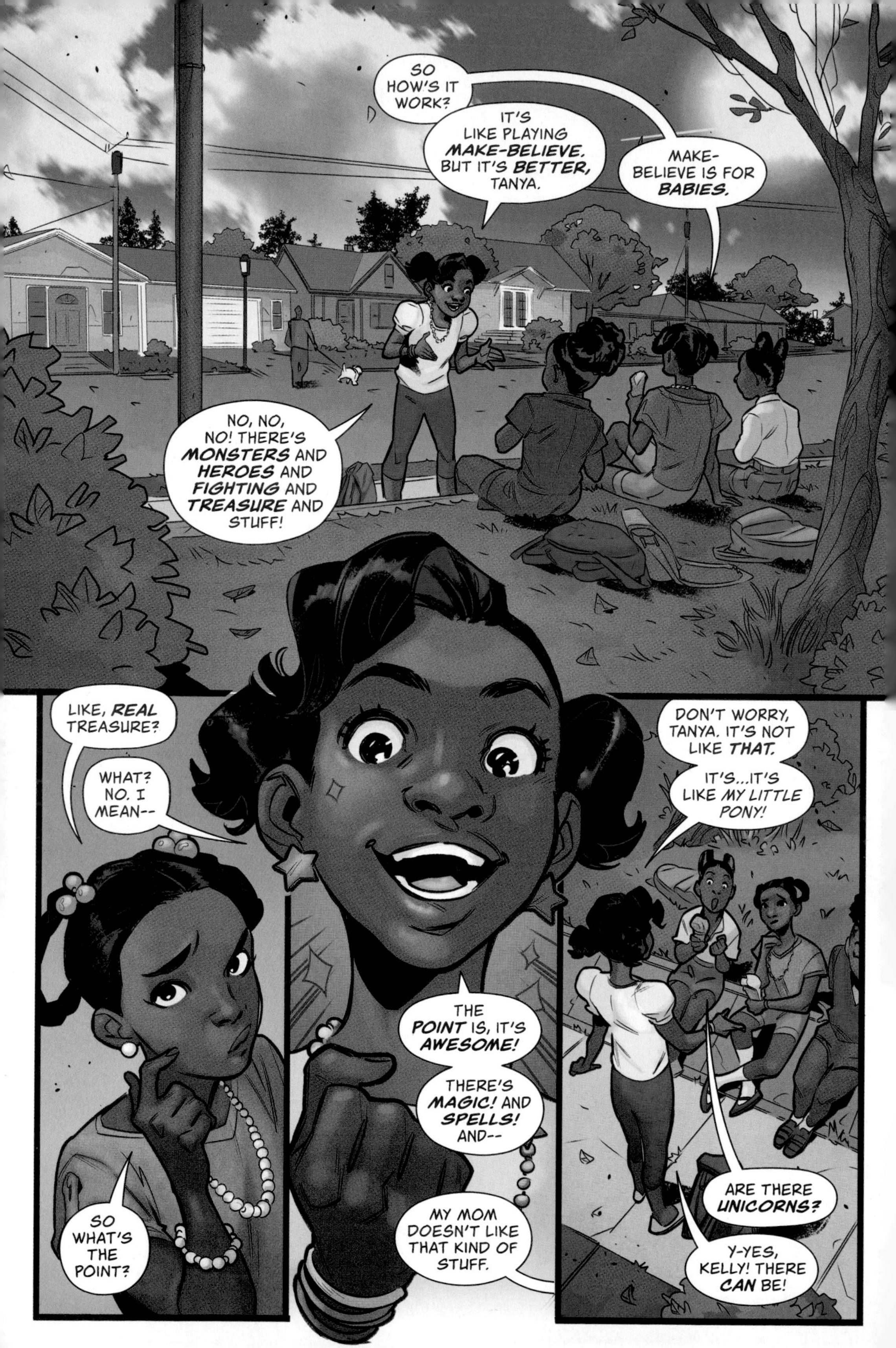
SO HOW'S IT WORK?
IT'S LIKE PLAYING MAKE-BELIEVE. BUT IT'S BETTER, TANYA.
MAKE-BELIEVE IS FOR BABIES.
NO, NO, NO! THERE'S MONSTERS AND HEROES AND FIGHTING AND TREASURE AND STUFF!
LIKE, REAL TREASURE?
WHAT? NO. I MEAN--
SO WHAT'S THE POINT?
THE POINT IS, IT'S AWESOME!
THERE'S MAGIC! AND SPELLS! AND--
MY MOM DOESN'T LIKE THAT KIND OF STUFF.
DON'T WORRY, TANYA. IT'S NOT LIKE THAT.
IT'S...IT'S LIKE MY LITTLE PONY!
ARE THERE UNICORNS?
Y-YES, KELLY! THERE CAN BE!

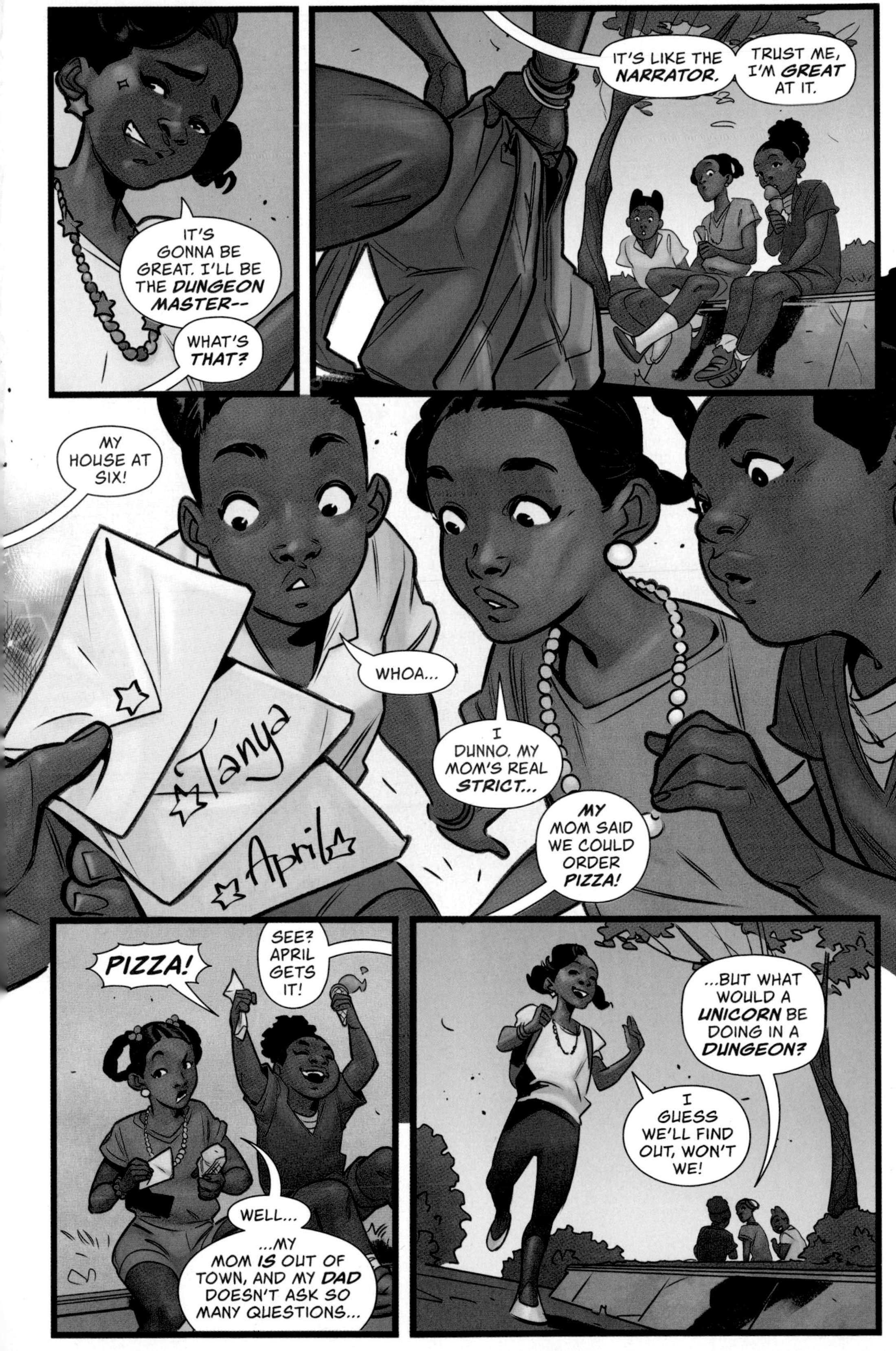

IT'S GONNA BE GREAT. I'LL BE THE DUNGEON MASTER--
WHAT'S THAT?
IT'S LIKE THE NARRATOR.
TRUST ME, I'M GREAT AT IT.
MY HOUSE AT SIX!
WHOA...
I DUNNO. MY MOM'S REAL STRICT...
MY MOM SAID WE COULD ORDER PIZZA!
Tanya
April
PIZZA!
SEE? APRIL GETS IT!
WELL...
...MY MOM IS OUT OF TOWN, AND MY DAD DOESN'T ASK SO MANY QUESTIONS...
...BUT WHAT WOULD A UNICORN BE DOING IN A DUNGEON?
I GUESS WE'LL FIND OUT, WON'T WE!

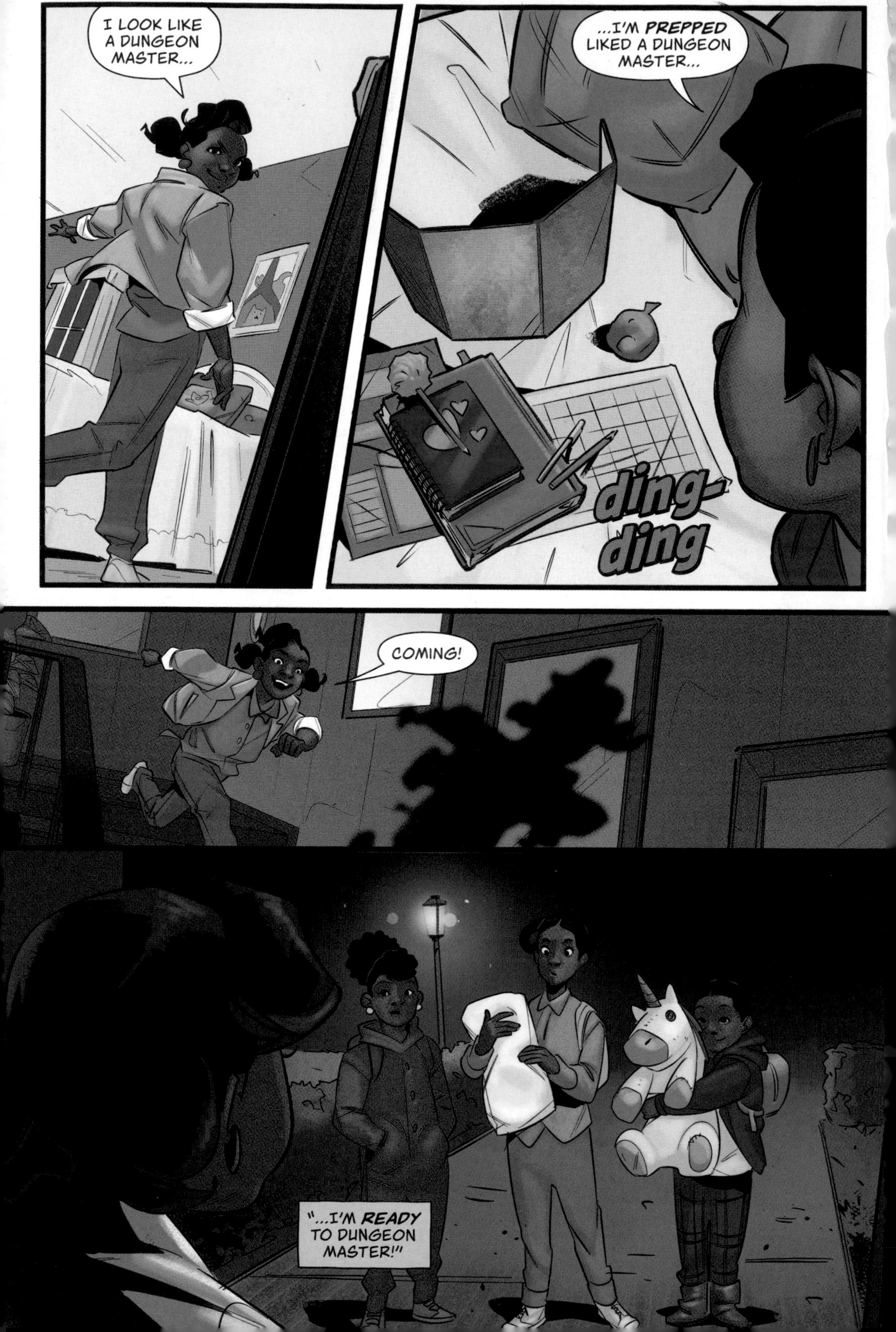
I LOOK LIKE A DUNGEON MASTER...
...I'M PREPPED LIKED A DUNGEON MASTER...
ding-ding
COMING!
"...I'M READY TO DUNGEON MASTER!"

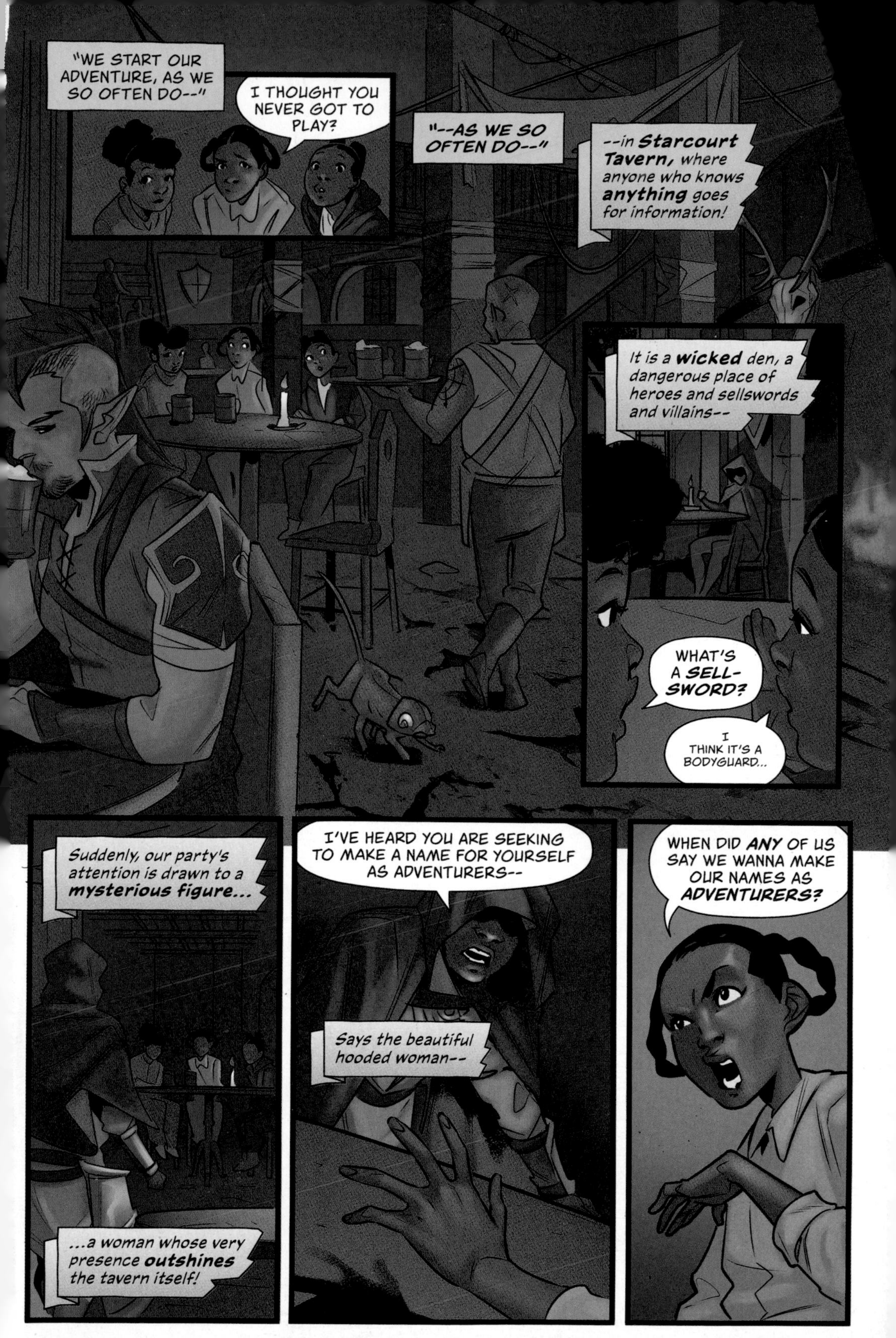
"WE START OUR ADVENTURE, AS WE SO OFTEN DO--"
I THOUGHT YOU NEVER GOT TO PLAY?
"--AS WE SO OFTEN DO--"
--in Starcourt Tavern, where anyone who knows anything goes for information!
It is a wicked den, a dangerous place of heroes and sellswords and villains--
WHAT'S A SELL-SWORD?
I THINK IT'S A BODYGUARD...
Suddenly, our party's attention is drawn to a mysterious figure...
...a woman whose very presence outshines the tavern itself!
I'VE HEARD YOU ARE SEEKING TO MAKE A NAME FOR YOURSELF AS ADVENTURERS--
Says the beautiful hooded woman--
WHEN DID ANY OF US SAY WE WANNA MAKE OUR NAMES AS ADVENTURERS?

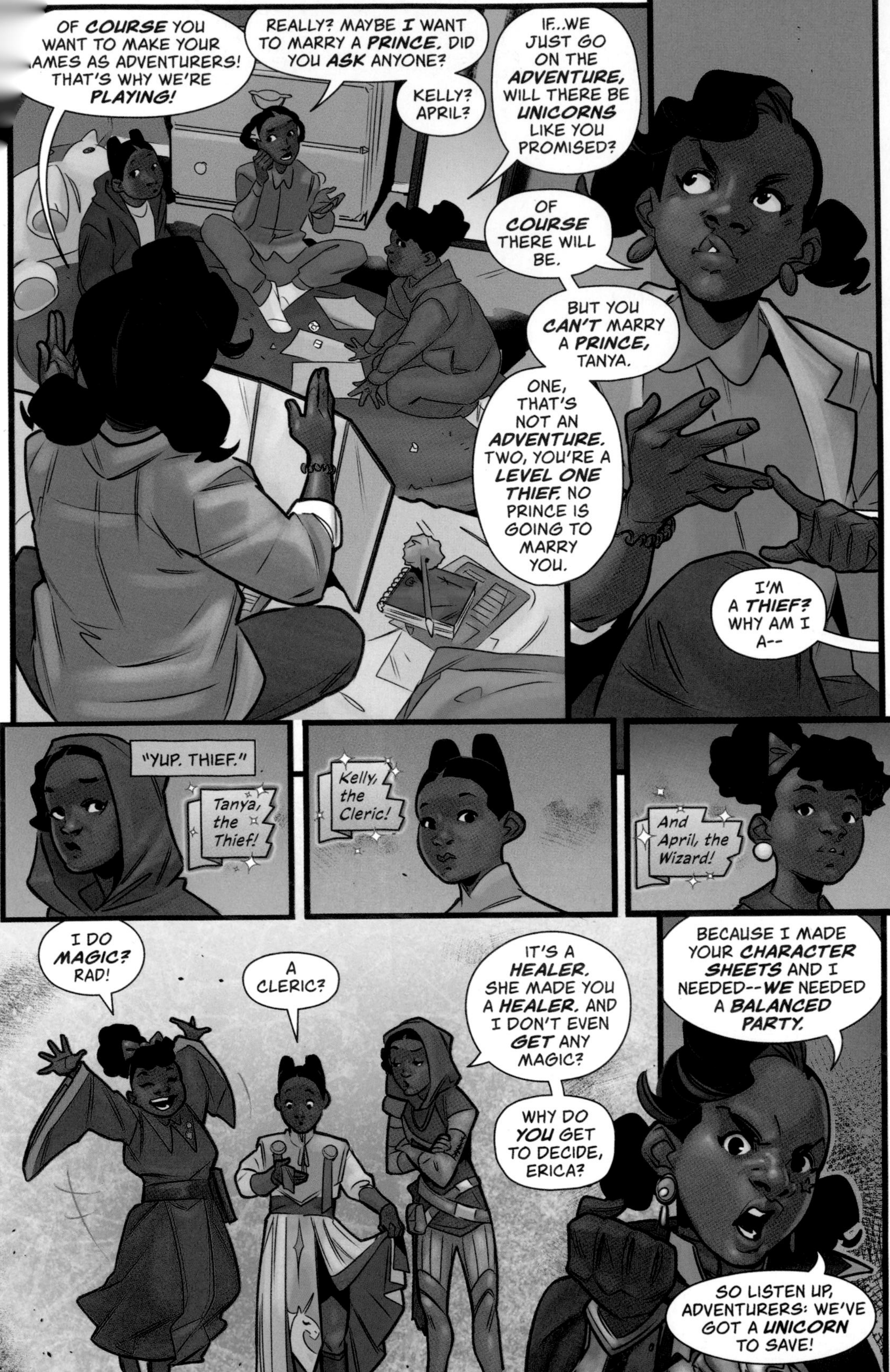

OF COURSE YOU WANT TO MAKE YOUR AMES AS ADVENTURERS! THAT'S WHY WE'RE PLAYING!
REALLY? MAYBE I WANT TO MARRY A PRINCE. DID YOU ASK ANYONE?
KELLY? APRIL?
IF...WE JUST GO ON THE ADVENTURE, WILL THERE BE UNICORNS LIKE YOU PROMISED?
OF COURSE THERE WILL BE.
BUT YOU CAN'T MARRY A PRINCE, TANYA.
ONE, THAT'S NOT AN ADVENTURE. TWO, YOU'RE A LEVEL ONE THIEF. NO PRINCE IS GOING TO MARRY YOU.
I'M A THIEF? WHY AM I A--
"YUP. THIEF."
Tanya, the Thief!
Kelly, the Cleric!
And April, the Wizard!
I DO MAGIC? RAD!
A CLERIC?
IT'S A HEALER. SHE MADE YOU A HEALER. AND I DON'T EVEN GET ANY MAGIC?
WHY DO YOU GET TO DECIDE, ERICA?
BECAUSE I MADE YOUR CHARACTER SHEETS AND I NEEDED--WE NEEDED A BALANCED PARTY.
SO LISTEN UP, ADVENTURERS: WE'VE GOT A UNICORN TO SAVE!

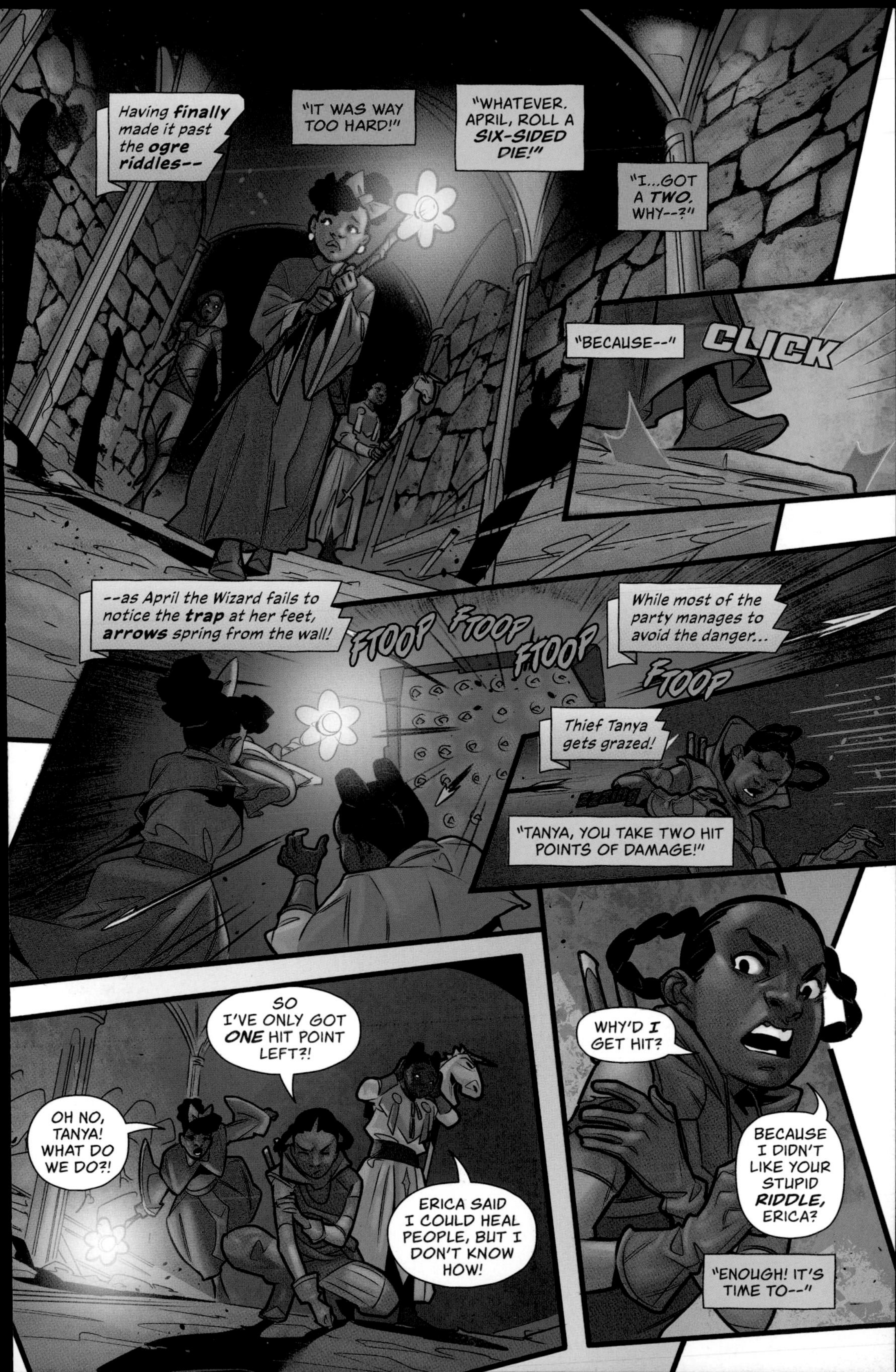
Having finally made it past the ogre riddles--
"IT WAS WAY TOO HARD!"
"WHATEVER. APRIL, ROLL A SIX-SIDED DIE!"
"I...GOT A TWO. WHY--?"
"BECAUSE--"
CLICK
--as April the Wizard fails to notice the trap at her feet, arrows spring from the wall!
FTOOP
FTOOP
FTOOP
While most of the party manages to avoid the danger...
FTOOP
Thief Tanya gets grazed!
"TANYA, YOU TAKE TWO HIT POINTS OF DAMAGE!"
SO I'VE ONLY GOT ONE HIT POINT LEFT?!
OH NO, TANYA! WHAT DO WE DO?!
ERICA SAID I COULD HEAL PEOPLE, BUT I DON'T KNOW HOW!
WHY'D I GET HIT?
BECAUSE I DIDN'T LIKE YOUR STUPID RIDDLE, ERICA?
"ENOUGH! IT'S TIME TO--"

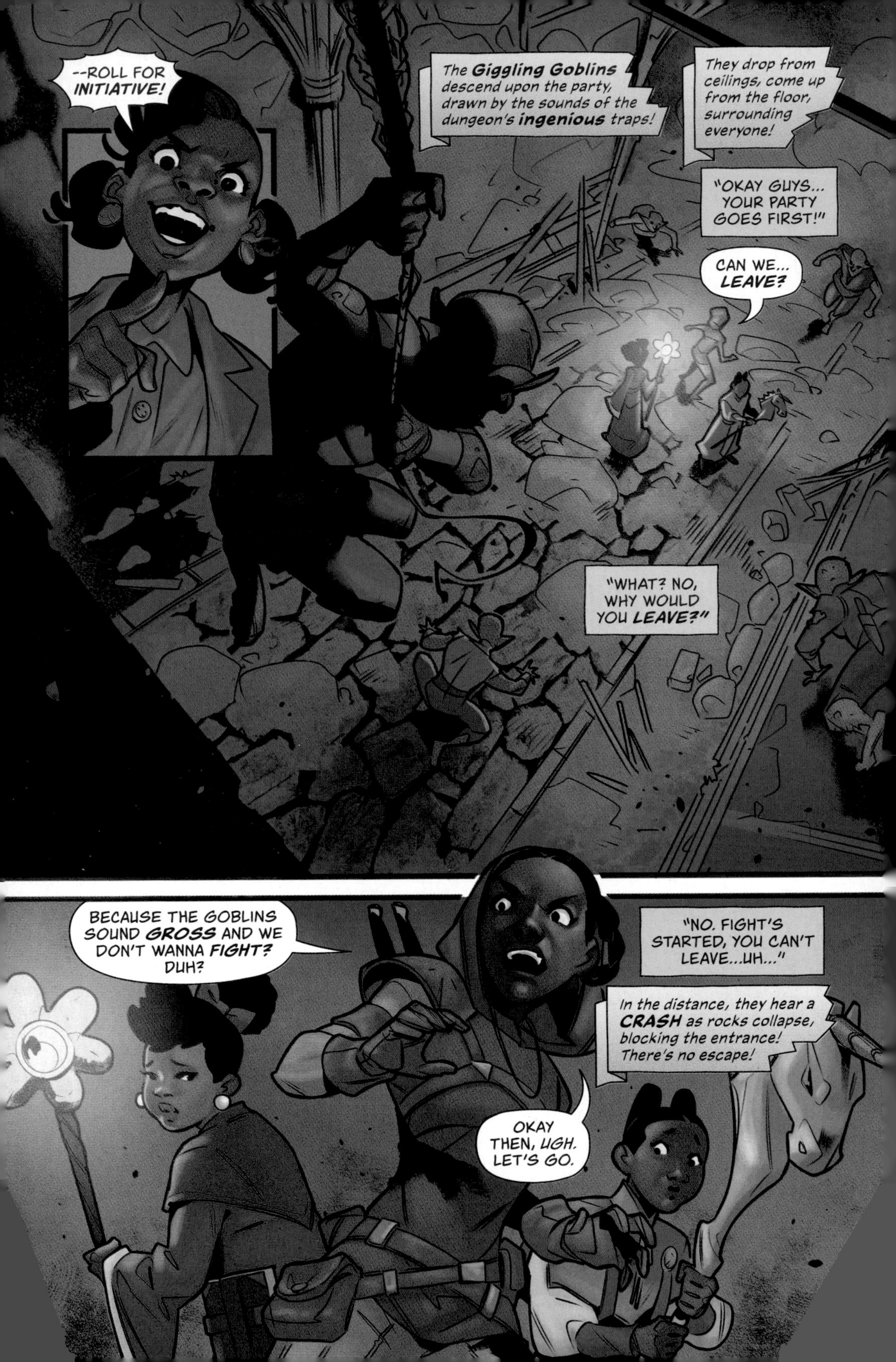
--ROLL FOR INITIATIVE!
The Giggling Goblins descend upon the party, drawn by the sounds of the dungeon's ingenious traps!
They drop from ceilings, come up from the floor, surrounding everyone!
"OKAY GUYS... YOUR PARTY GOES FIRST!"
CAN WE... LEAVE?
"WHAT? NO, WHY WOULD YOU LEAVE?"
BECAUSE THE GOBLINS SOUND GROSS AND WE DON'T WANNA FIGHT? DUH?
"NO. FIGHT'S STARTED, YOU CAN'T LEAVE...UH..."
In the distance, they hear a CRASH as rocks collapse, blocking the entrance! There's no escape!
OKAY THEN, UGH. LET'S GO.

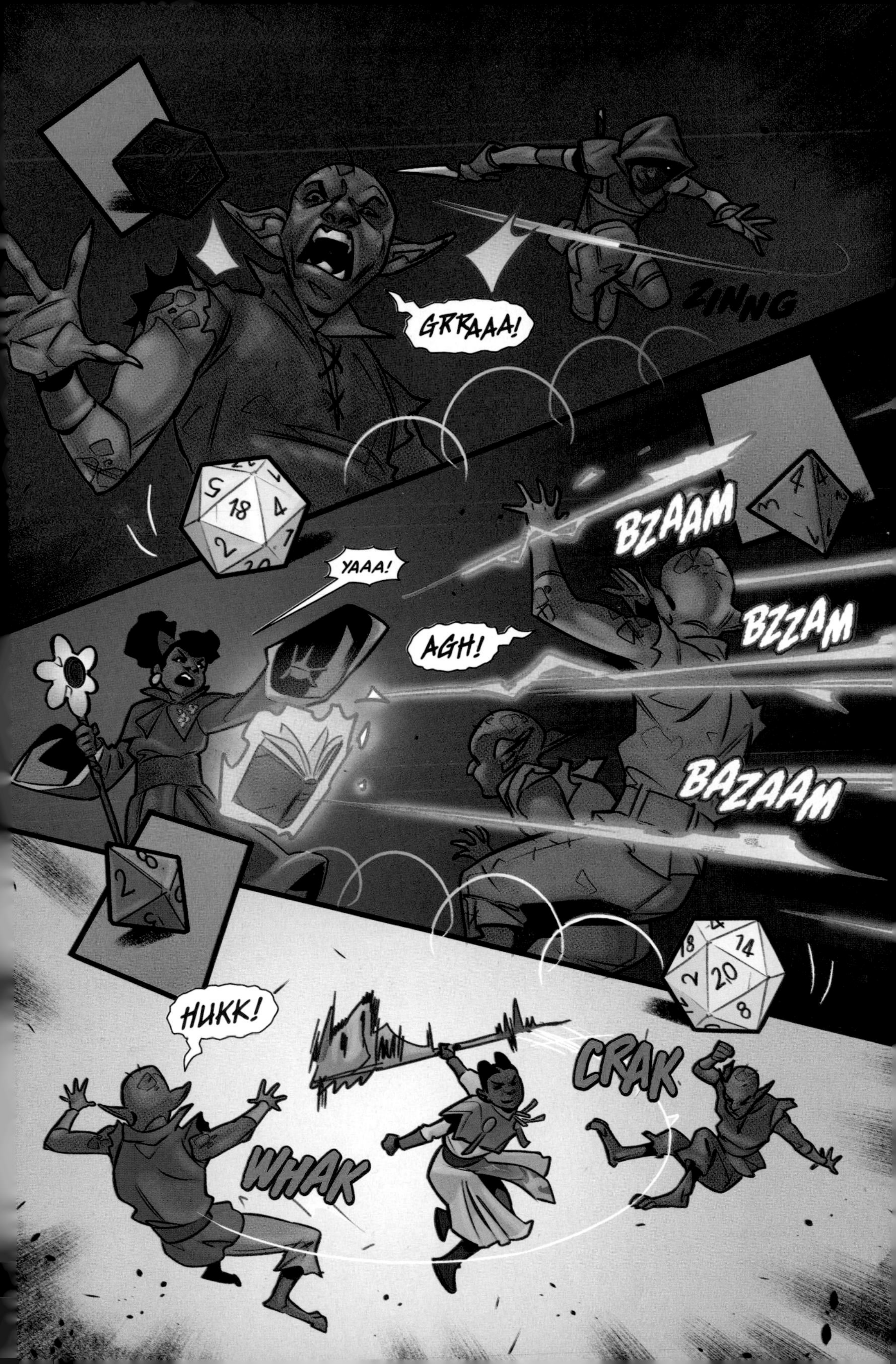
GRRAAA!
ZINNG
YAAA!
BZAAM
AGH!
BZZAM
BAZAAM
HUKK!
CRAK
WHAK

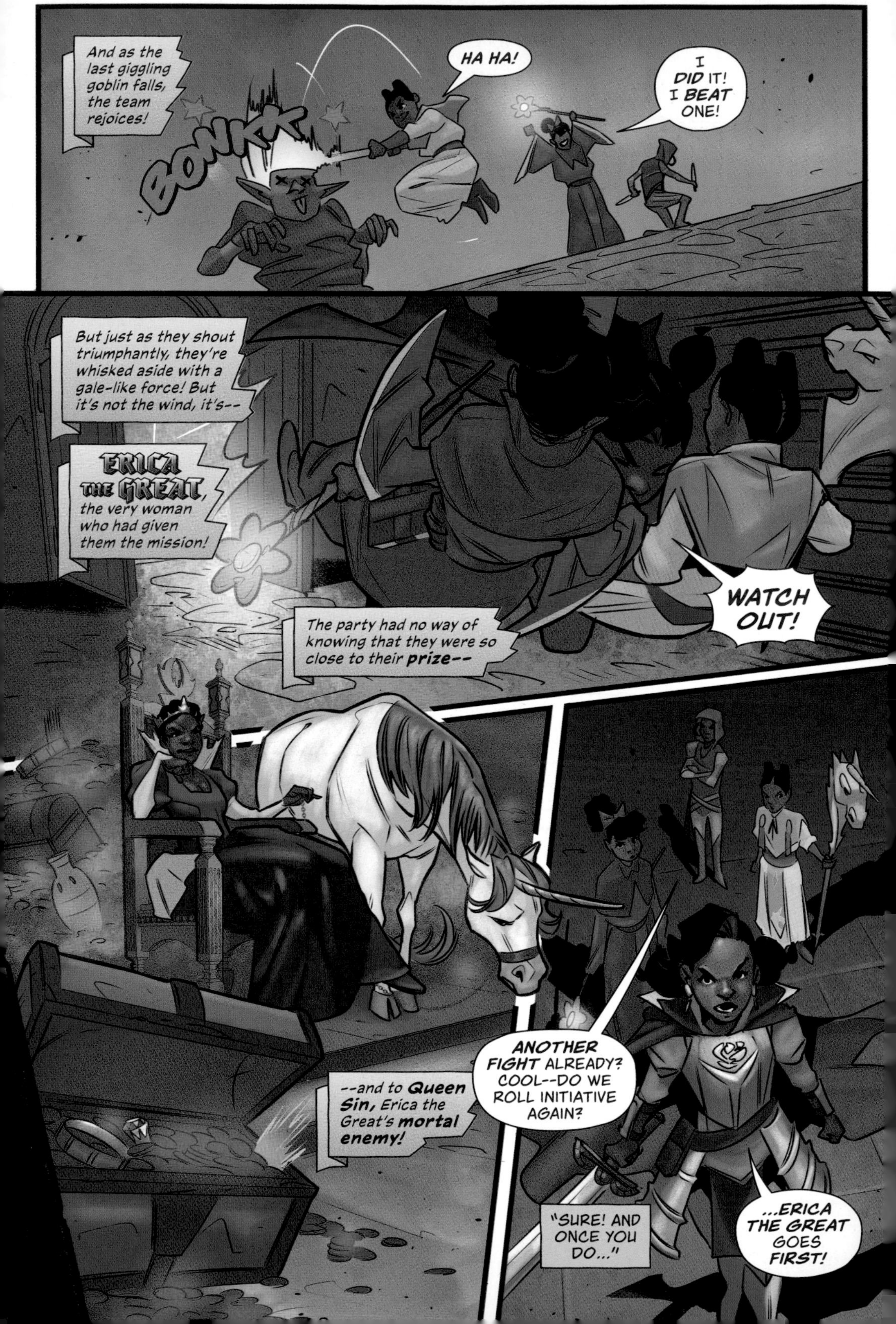
And as the last giggling goblin falls, the team rejoices!
BONKK
HA HA!
I DID IT! I BEAT ONE!
But just as they shout triumphantly, they're whisked aside with a gale-like force! But it's not the wind, it's--
ERICA THE GREAT, the very woman who had given them the mission!
WATCH OUT!
The party had no way of knowing that they were so close to their prize--
--and to Queen Sin, Erica the Great's mortal enemy!
ANOTHER FIGHT ALREADY? COOL--DO WE ROLL INITIATIVE AGAIN?
"SURE! AND ONCE YOU DO..."
...ERICA THE GREAT GOES FIRST!

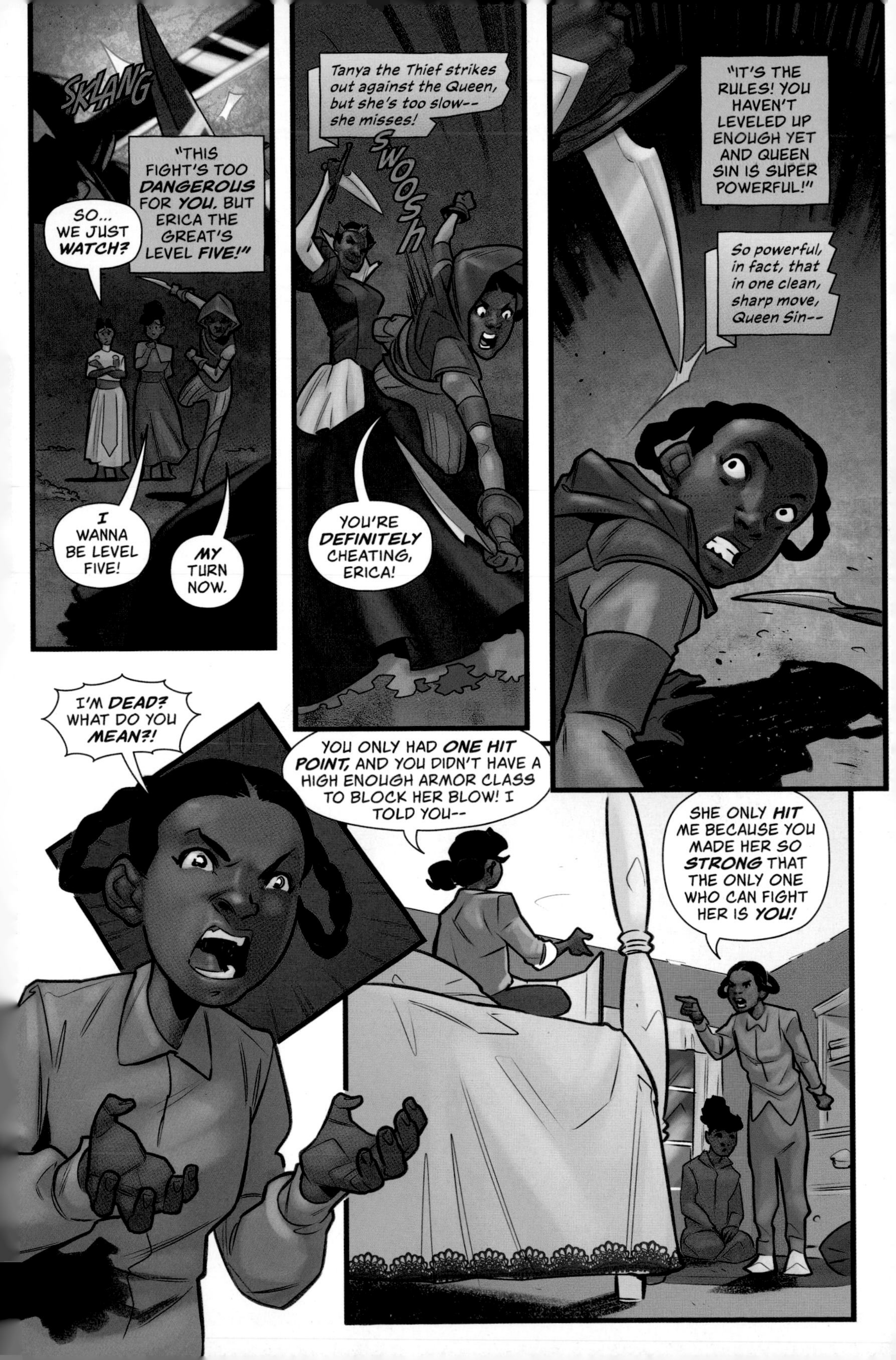
SKLANG
"THIS FIGHT'S TOO **DANGEROUS** FOR **YOU.** BUT ERICA THE GREAT'S LEVEL **FIVE!**"
SO... WE JUST **WATCH?**
I WANNA BE LEVEL FIVE!
MY TURN NOW.
Tanya the Thief strikes out against the Queen, but she's too slow-- she misses!
SWOOSH
YOU'RE **DEFINITELY** CHEATING, ERICA!
"IT'S THE RULES! YOU HAVEN'T LEVELED UP ENOUGH YET AND QUEEN SIN IS SUPER POWERFUL!"
So powerful, in fact, that in one clean, sharp move, Queen Sin--
I'M **DEAD?** WHAT DO YOU **MEAN?!**
YOU ONLY HAD **ONE HIT POINT,** AND YOU DIDN'T HAVE A HIGH ENOUGH ARMOR CLASS TO BLOCK HER BLOW! I TOLD YOU--
SHE ONLY **HIT** ME BECAUSE YOU MADE HER SO **STRONG** THAT THE ONLY ONE WHO CAN FIGHT HER IS **YOU!**

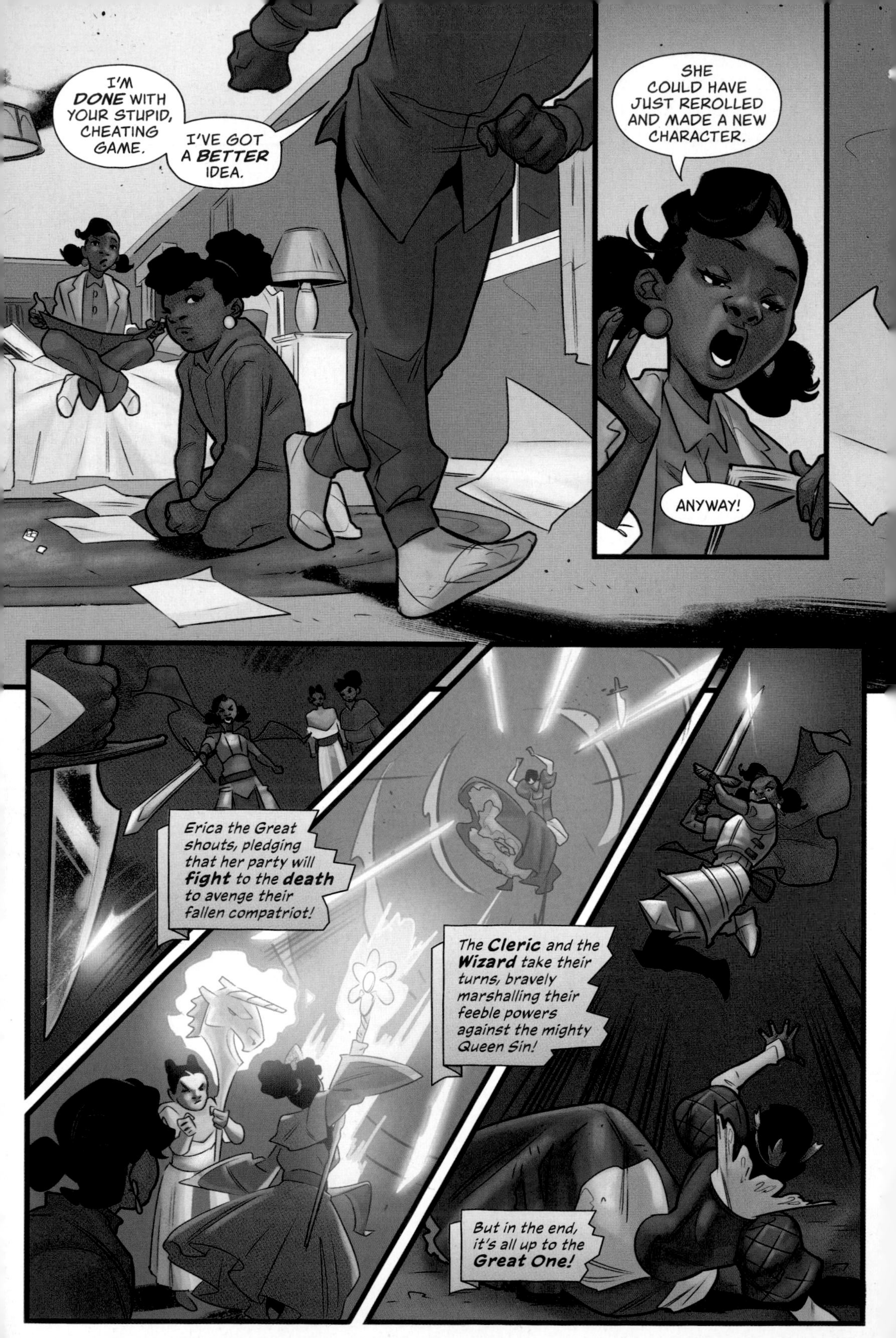
I'M DONE WITH YOUR STUPID, CHEATING GAME.
I'VE GOT A BETTER IDEA.
SHE COULD HAVE JUST REROLLED AND MADE A NEW CHARACTER.
ANYWAY!
Erica the Great shouts, pledging that her party will fight to the death to avenge their fallen compatriot!
The Cleric and the Wizard take their turns, bravely marshalling their feeble powers against the mighty Queen Sin!
But in the end, it's all up to the Great One!

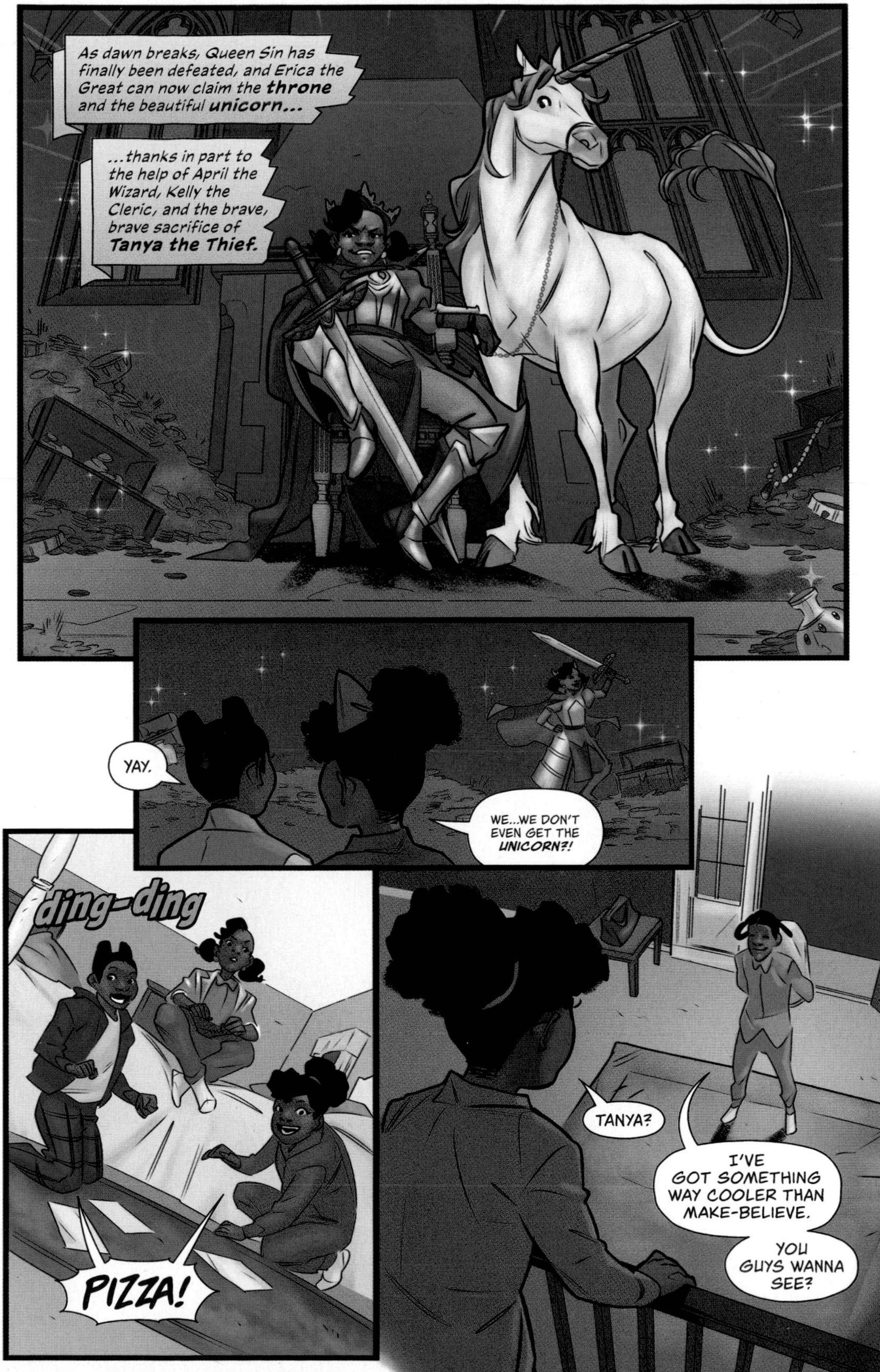
As dawn breaks, Queen Sin has finally been defeated, and Erica the Great can now claim the **throne** and the beautiful **unicorn...**
...thanks in part to the help of April the Wizard, Kelly the Cleric, and the brave, brave sacrifice of **Tanya the Thief.**
YAY.
WE...WE DON'T EVEN GET THE *UNICORN?!*
ding-ding
PIZZA!
TANYA?
I'VE GOT SOMETHING WAY COOLER THAN MAKE-BELIEVE.
YOU GUYS WANNA SEE?

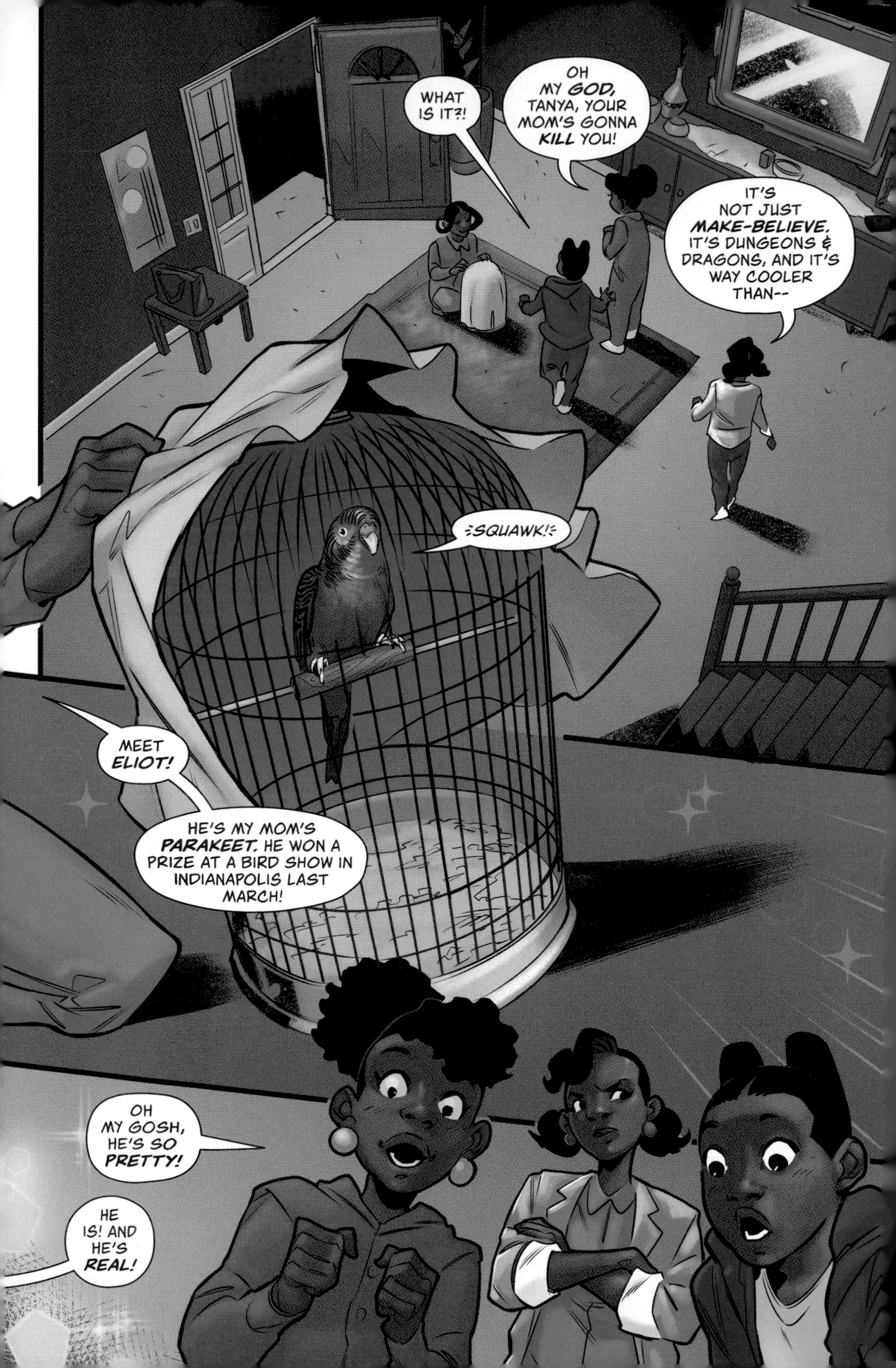
WHAT IS IT?!
OH MY GOD, TANYA, YOUR MOM'S GONNA KILL YOU!
IT'S NOT JUST MAKE-BELIEVE. IT'S DUNGEONS & DRAGONS, AND IT'S WAY COOLER THAN--
SQUAWK!
MEET ELIOT!
HE'S MY MOM'S PARAKEET. HE WON A PRIZE AT A BIRD SHOW IN INDIANAPOLIS LAST MARCH!
OH MY GOSH, HE'S SO PRETTY!
HE IS! AND HE'S REAL!

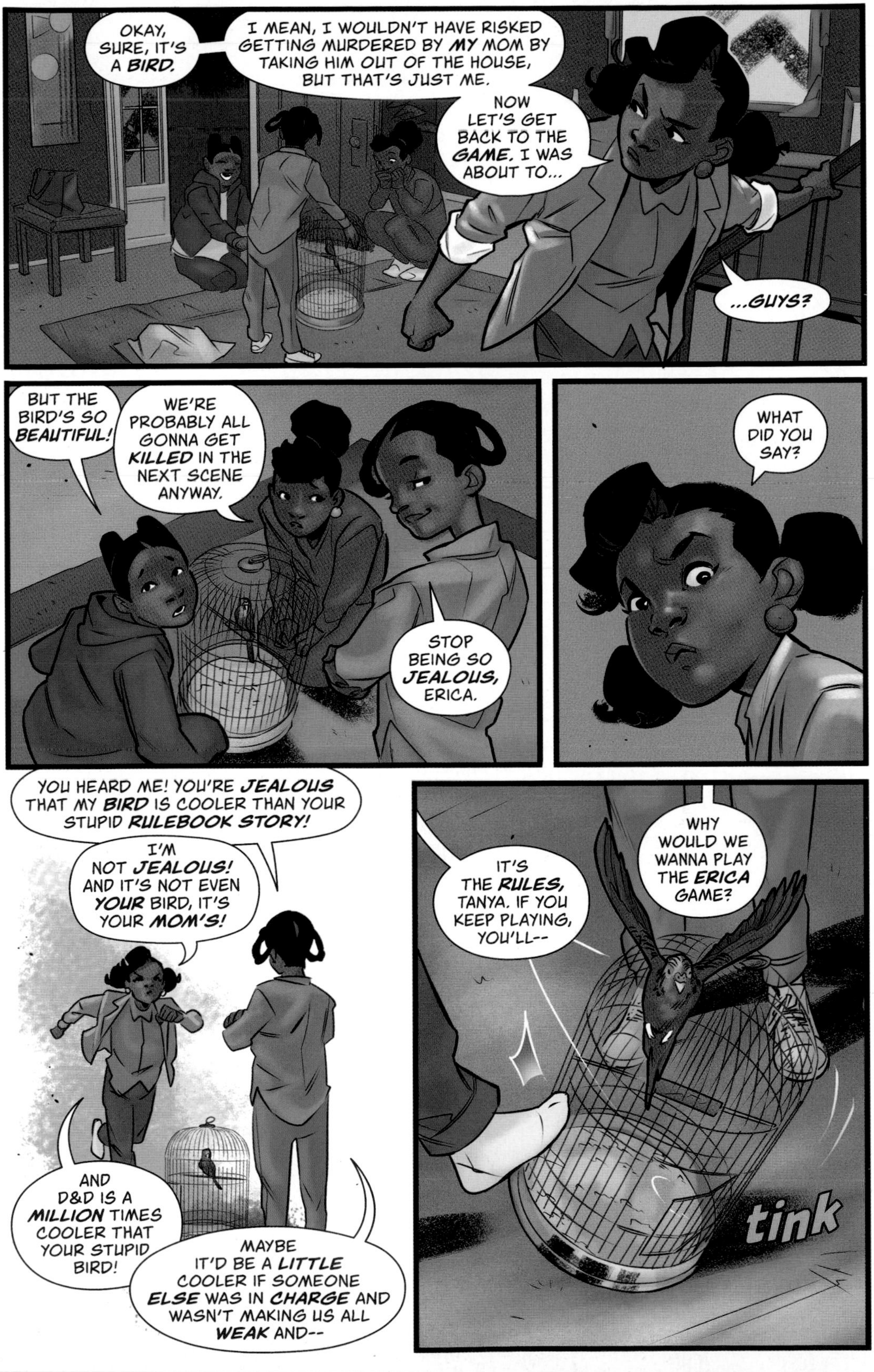
OKAY, SURE, IT'S A BIRD.
I MEAN, I WOULDN'T HAVE RISKED GETTING MURDERED BY MY MOM BY TAKING HIM OUT OF THE HOUSE, BUT THAT'S JUST ME.
NOW LET'S GET BACK TO THE GAME. I WAS ABOUT TO...
...GUYS?
BUT THE BIRD'S SO BEAUTIFUL!
WE'RE PROBABLY ALL GONNA GET KILLED IN THE NEXT SCENE ANYWAY.
STOP BEING SO JEALOUS, ERICA.
WHAT DID YOU SAY?
YOU HEARD ME! YOU'RE JEALOUS THAT MY BIRD IS COOLER THAN YOUR STUPID RULEBOOK STORY!
I'M NOT JEALOUS! AND IT'S NOT EVEN YOUR BIRD, IT'S YOUR MOM'S!
AND D&D IS A MILLION TIMES COOLER THAT YOUR STUPID BIRD!
MAYBE IT'D BE A LITTLE COOLER IF SOMEONE ELSE WAS IN CHARGE AND WASN'T MAKING US ALL WEAK AND--
IT'S THE RULES, TANYA. IF YOU KEEP PLAYING, YOU'LL--
WHY WOULD WE WANNA PLAY THE ERICA GAME?
tink

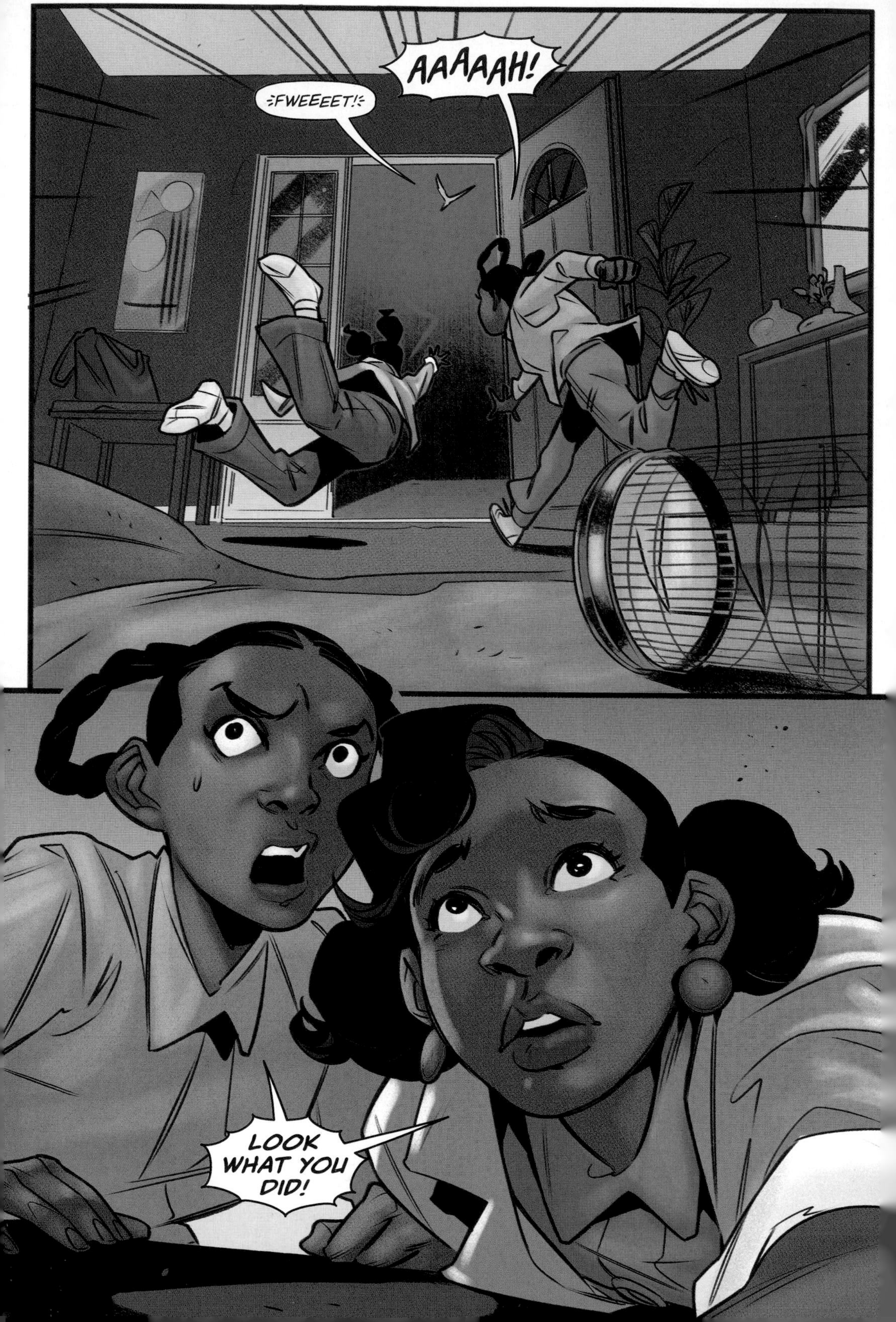
FWEEEET!
AAAAAH!
LOOK WHAT YOU DID!

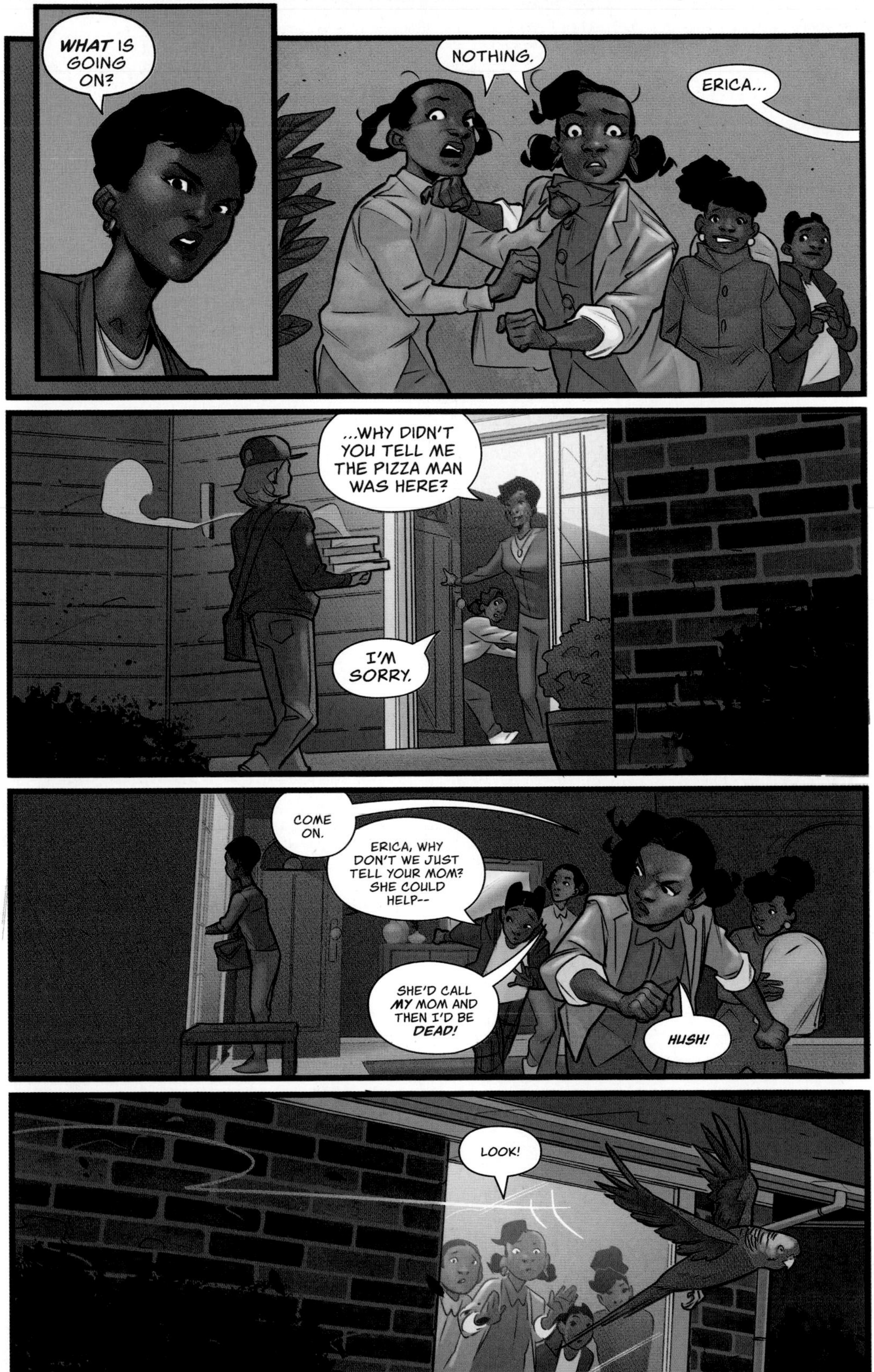
WHAT IS GOING ON?
NOTHING.
ERICA...
...WHY DIDN'T YOU TELL ME THE PIZZA MAN WAS HERE?
I'M SORRY.
COME ON.
ERICA, WHY DON'T WE JUST TELL YOUR MOM? SHE COULD HELP--
SHE'D CALL MY MOM AND THEN I'D BE DEAD!
HUSH!
LOOK!

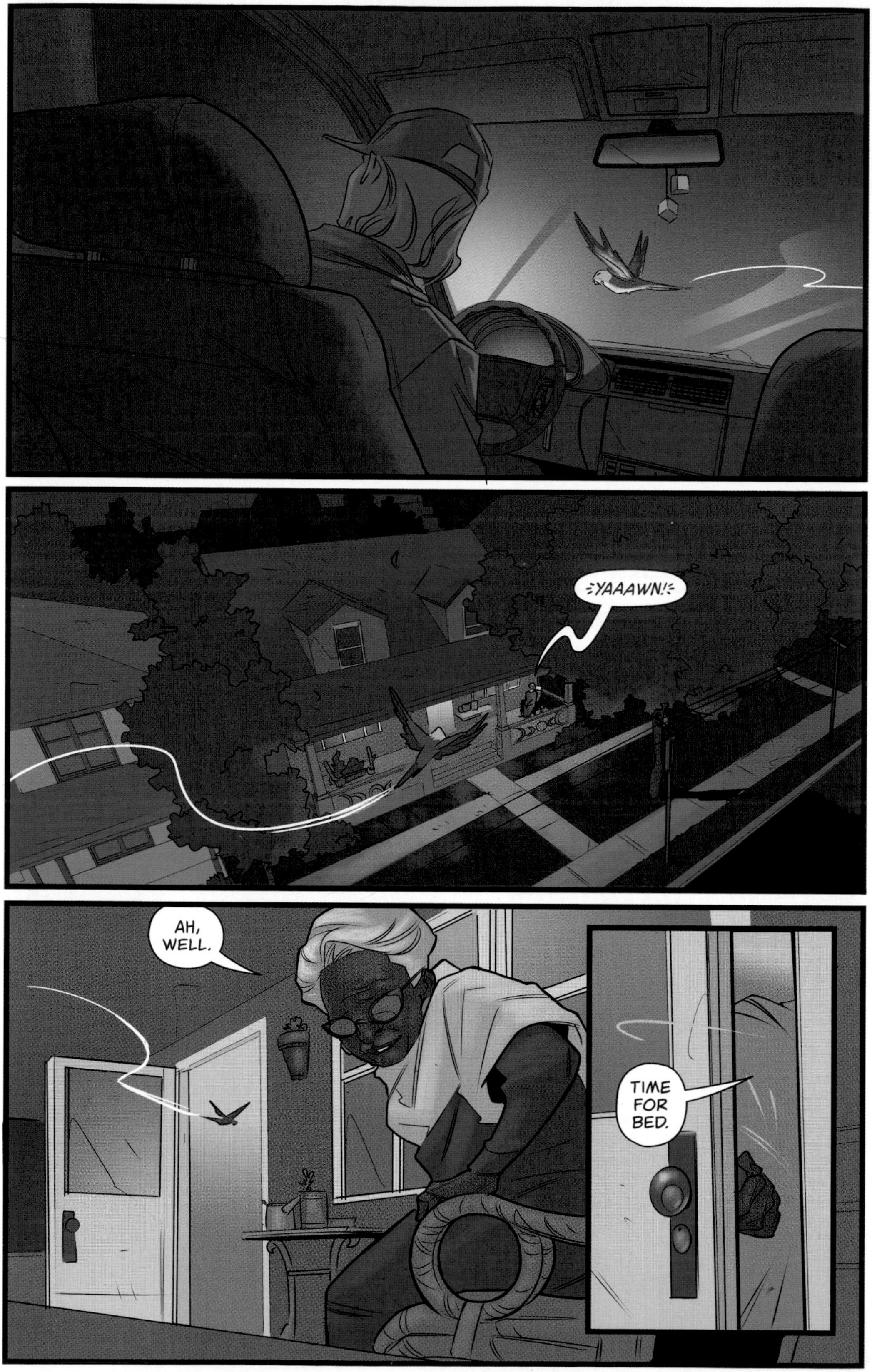
YAAAWN!
AH, WELL.
TIME FOR BED.

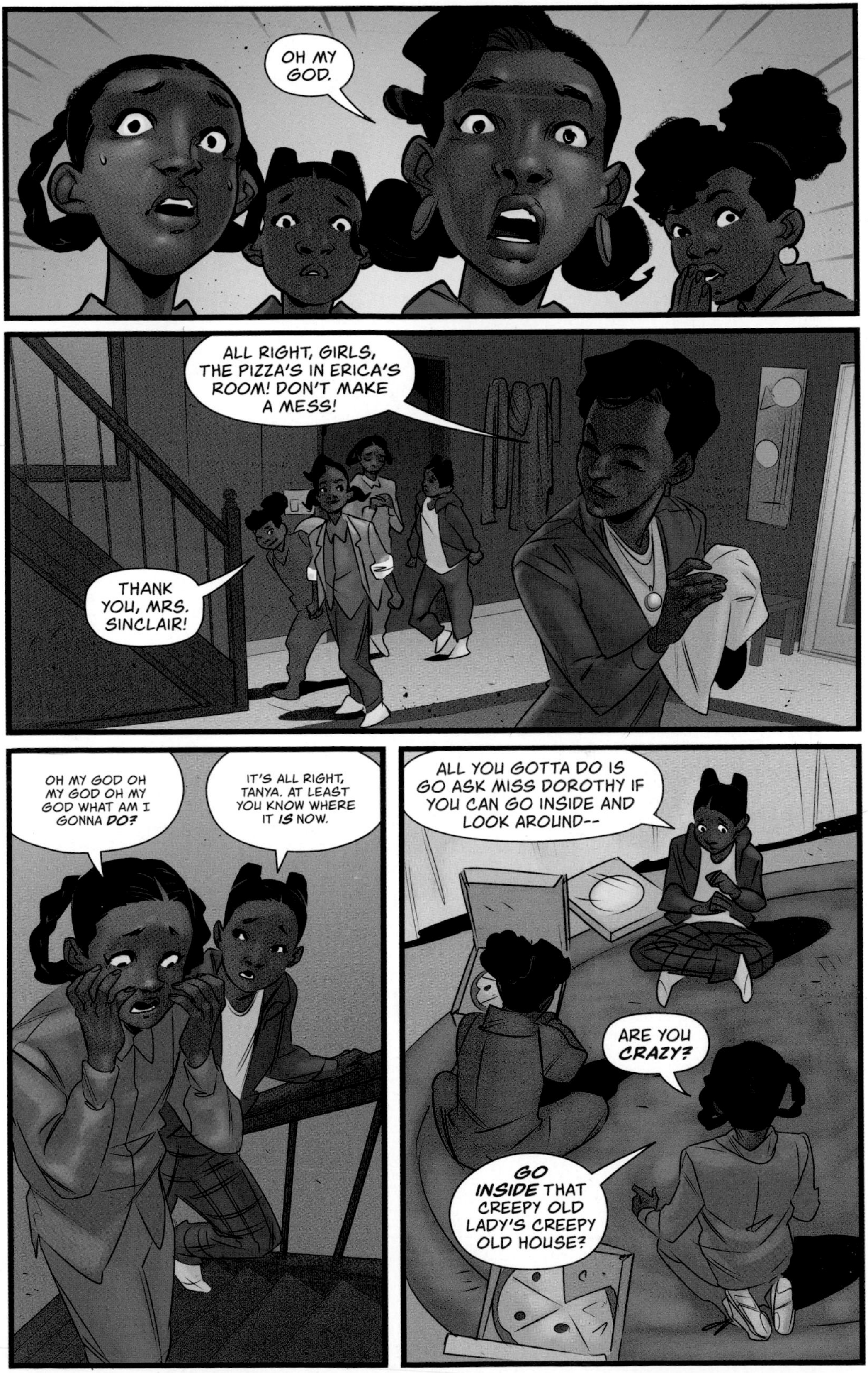
OH MY GOD.
ALL RIGHT, GIRLS, THE PIZZA'S IN ERICA'S ROOM! DON'T MAKE A MESS!
THANK YOU, MRS. SINCLAIR!
OH MY GOD OH MY GOD OH MY GOD WHAT AM I GONNA DO?
IT'S ALL RIGHT, TANYA. AT LEAST YOU KNOW WHERE IT IS NOW.
ALL YOU GOTTA DO IS GO ASK MISS DOROTHY IF YOU CAN GO INSIDE AND LOOK AROUND--
ARE YOU CRAZY?
GO INSIDE THAT CREEPY OLD LADY'S CREEPY OLD HOUSE?

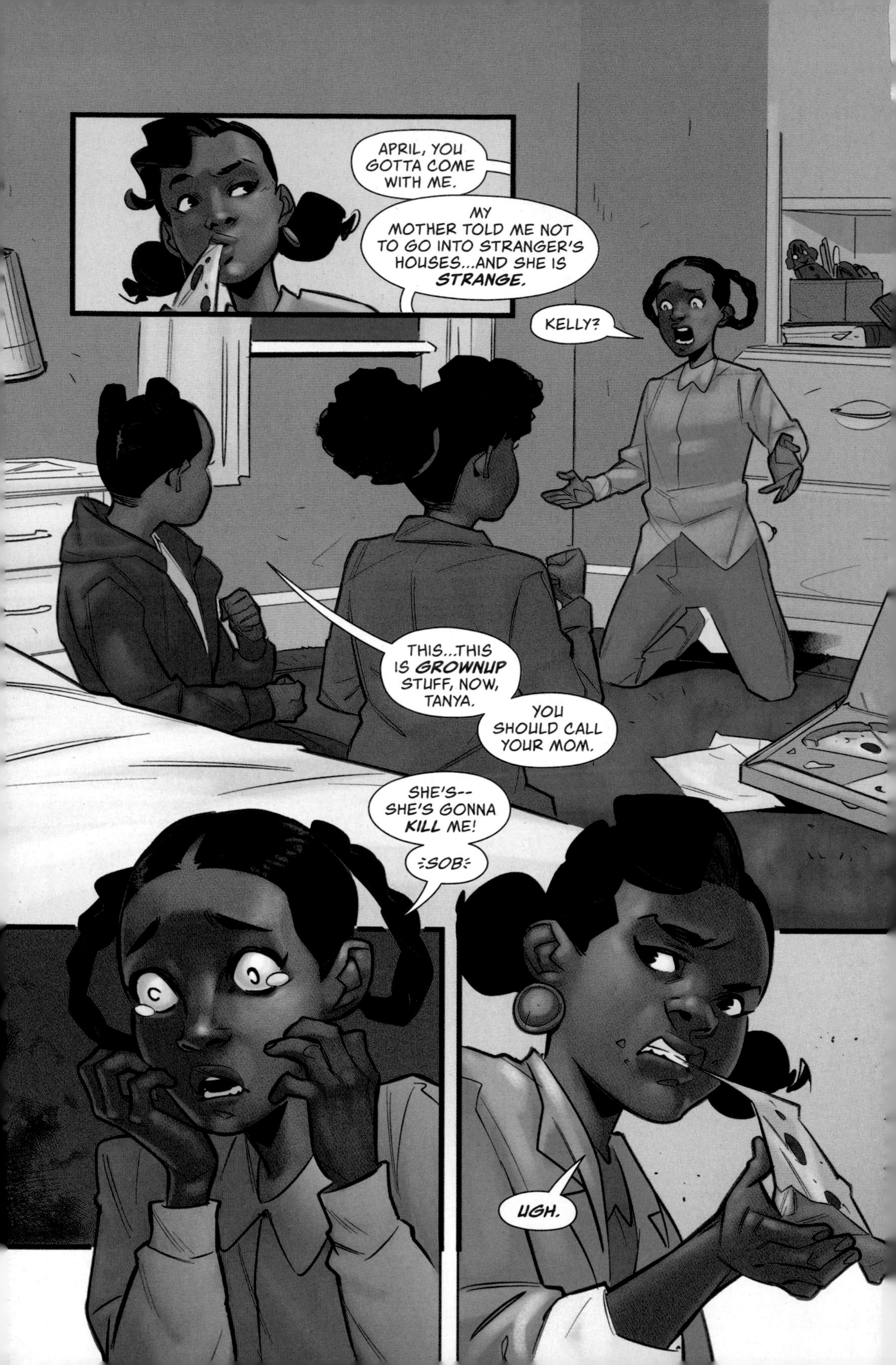
APRIL, YOU GOTTA COME WITH ME.
MY MOTHER TOLD ME NOT TO GO INTO STRANGER'S HOUSES...AND SHE IS STRANGE.
KELLY?
THIS...THIS IS GROWNUP STUFF, NOW, TANYA.
YOU SHOULD CALL YOUR MOM.
SHE'S-- SHE'S GONNA KILL ME!
SOB
UGH.

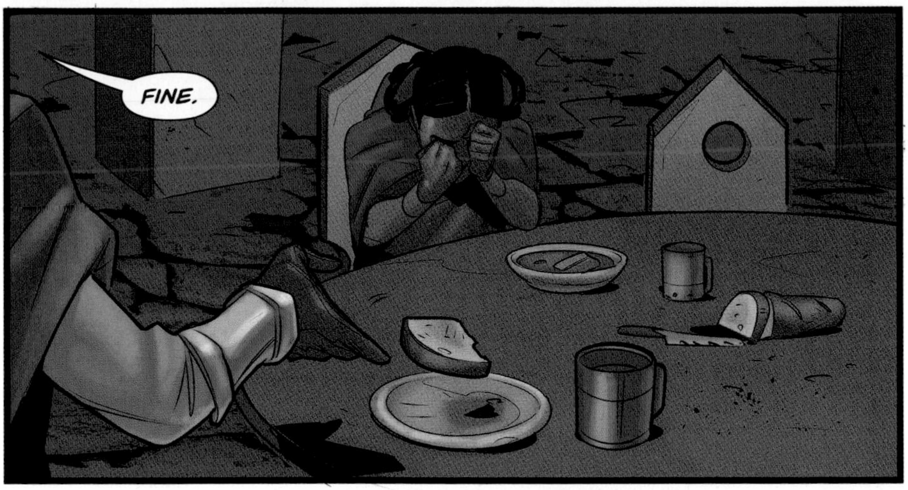
FINE.

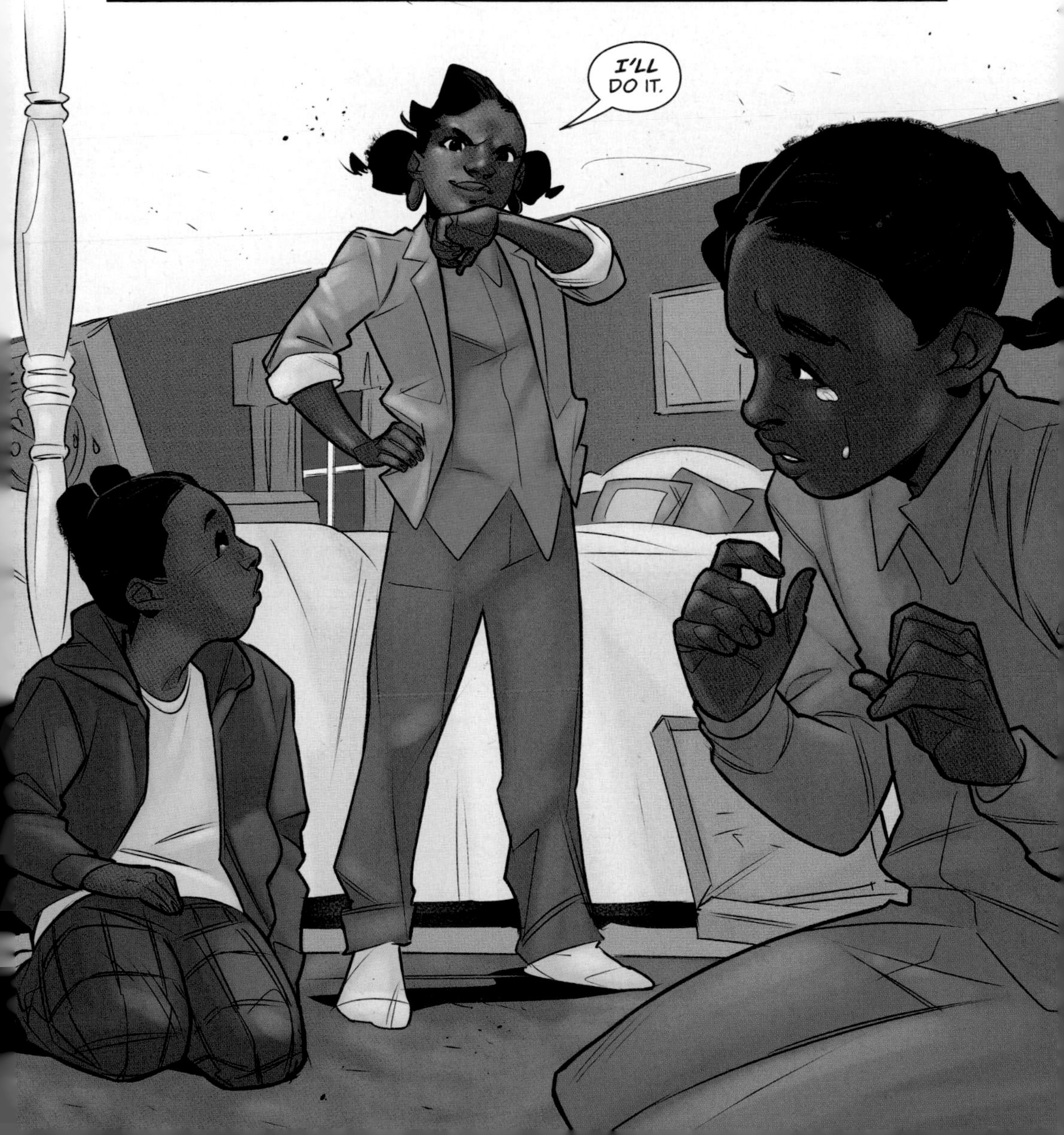
I'LL DO IT.

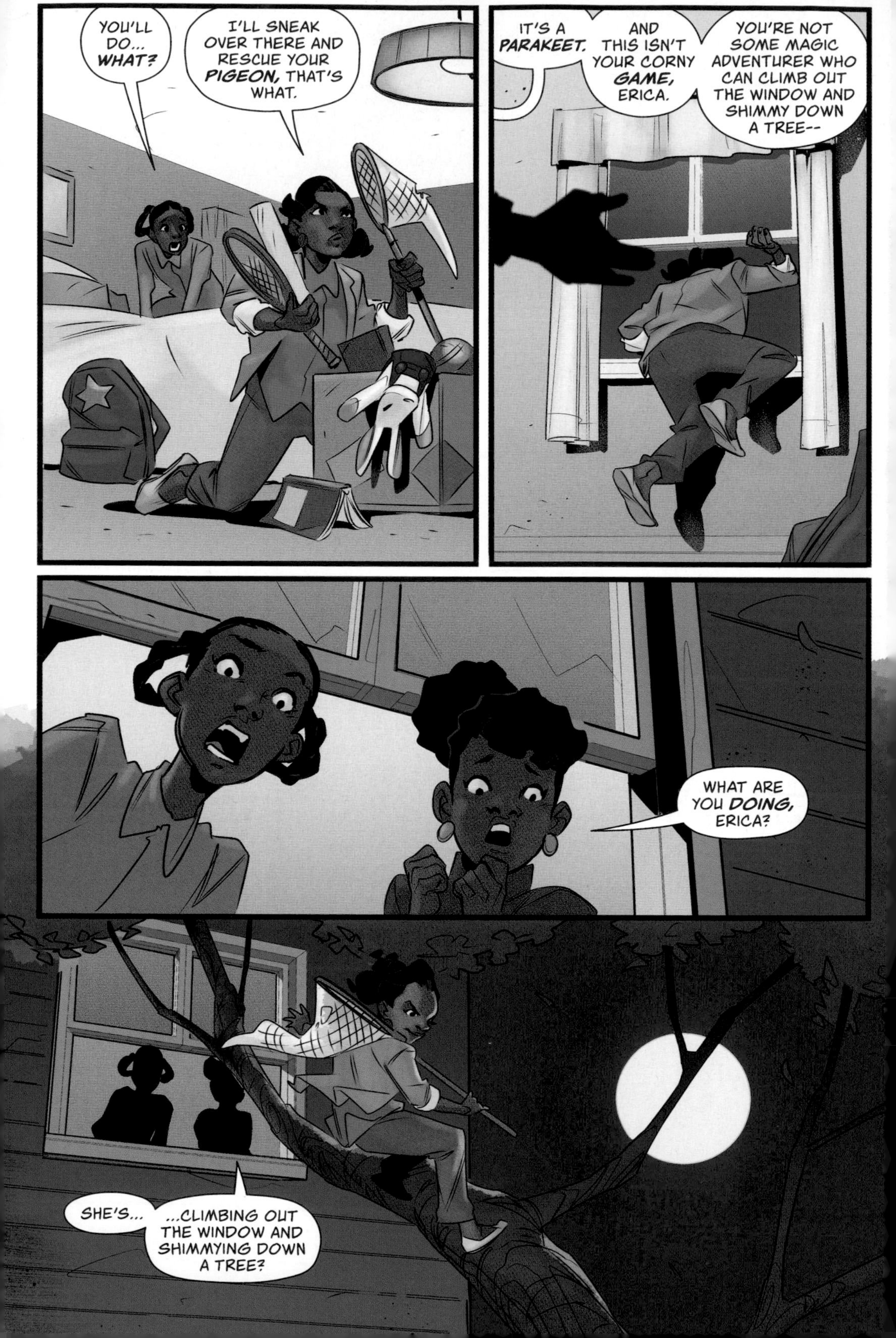
YOU'LL DO... WHAT?
I'LL SNEAK OVER THERE AND RESCUE YOUR PIGEON, THAT'S WHAT.
IT'S A PARAKEET.
AND THIS ISN'T YOUR CORNY GAME, ERICA.
YOU'RE NOT SOME MAGIC ADVENTURER WHO CAN CLIMB OUT THE WINDOW AND SHIMMY DOWN A TREE--
WHAT ARE YOU DOING, ERICA?
SHE'S...
...CLIMBING OUT THE WINDOW AND SHIMMYING DOWN A TREE?

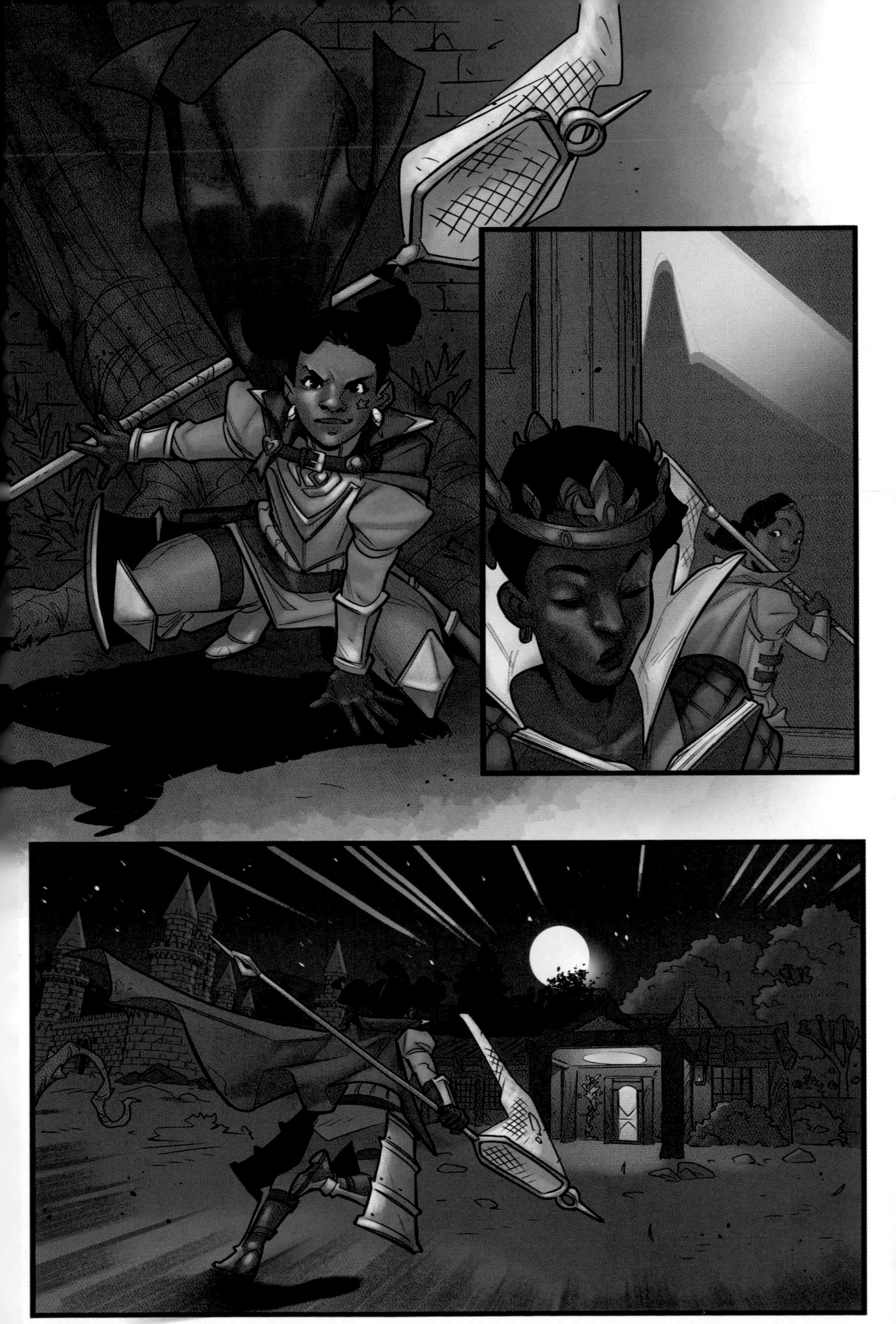

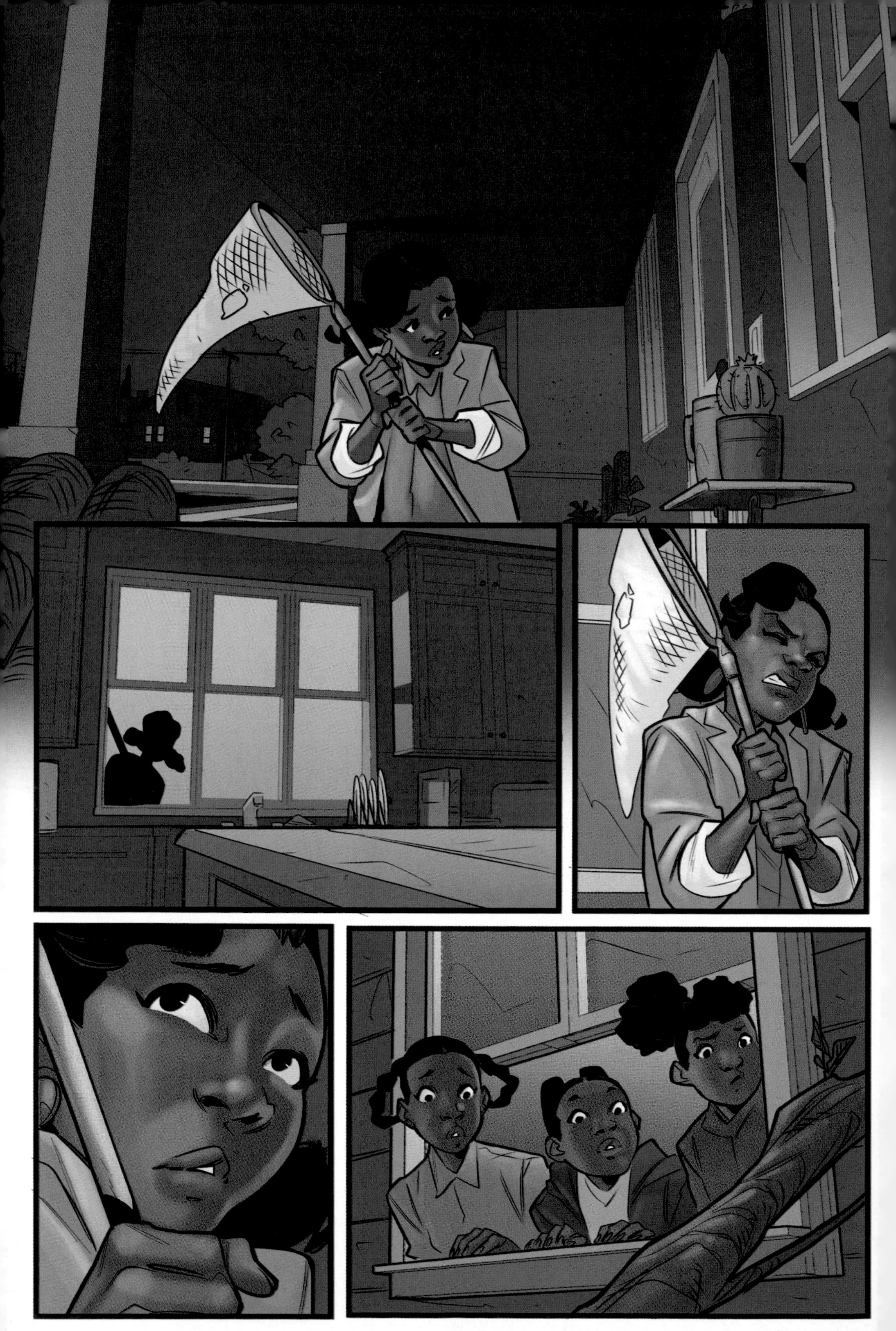

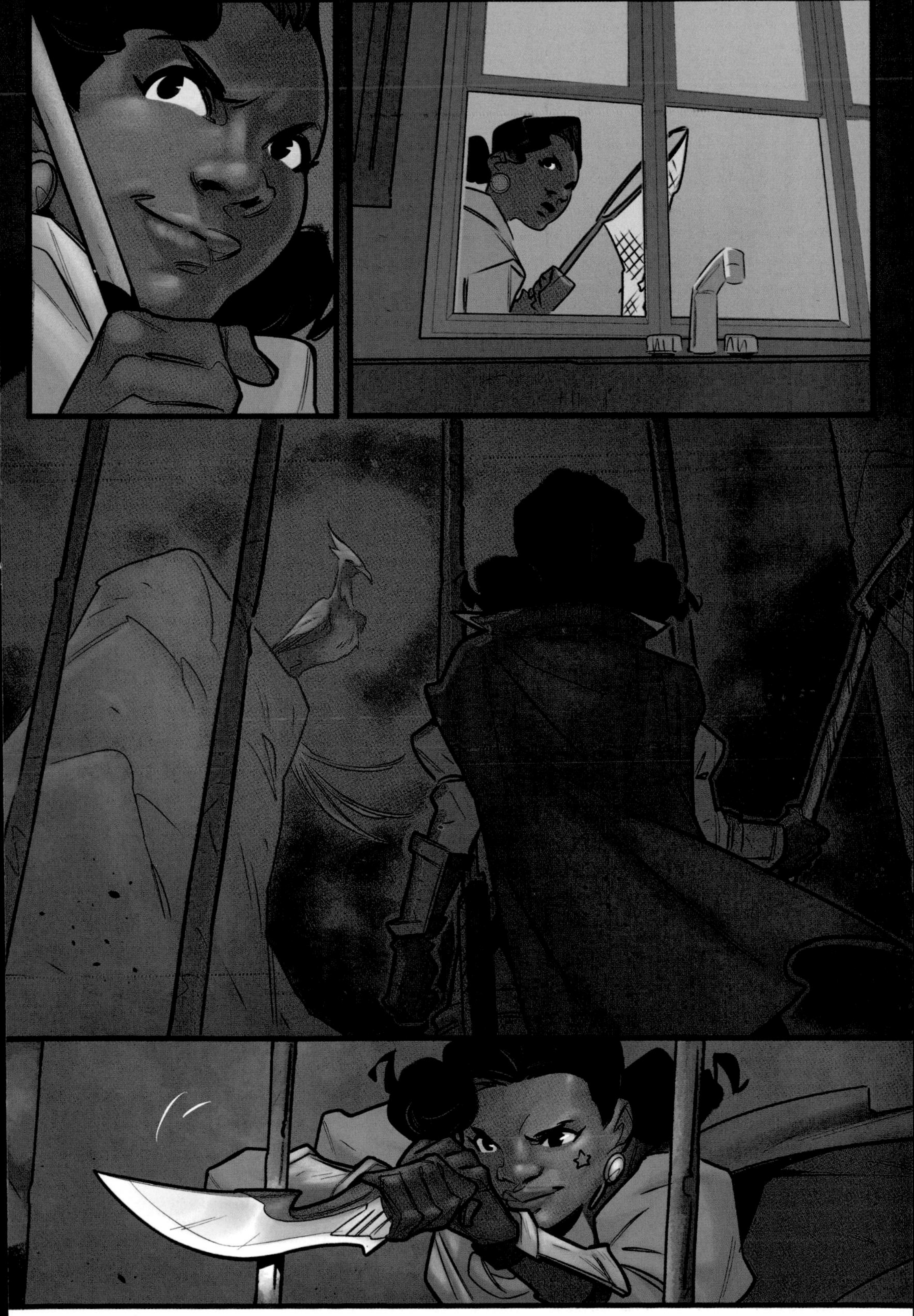

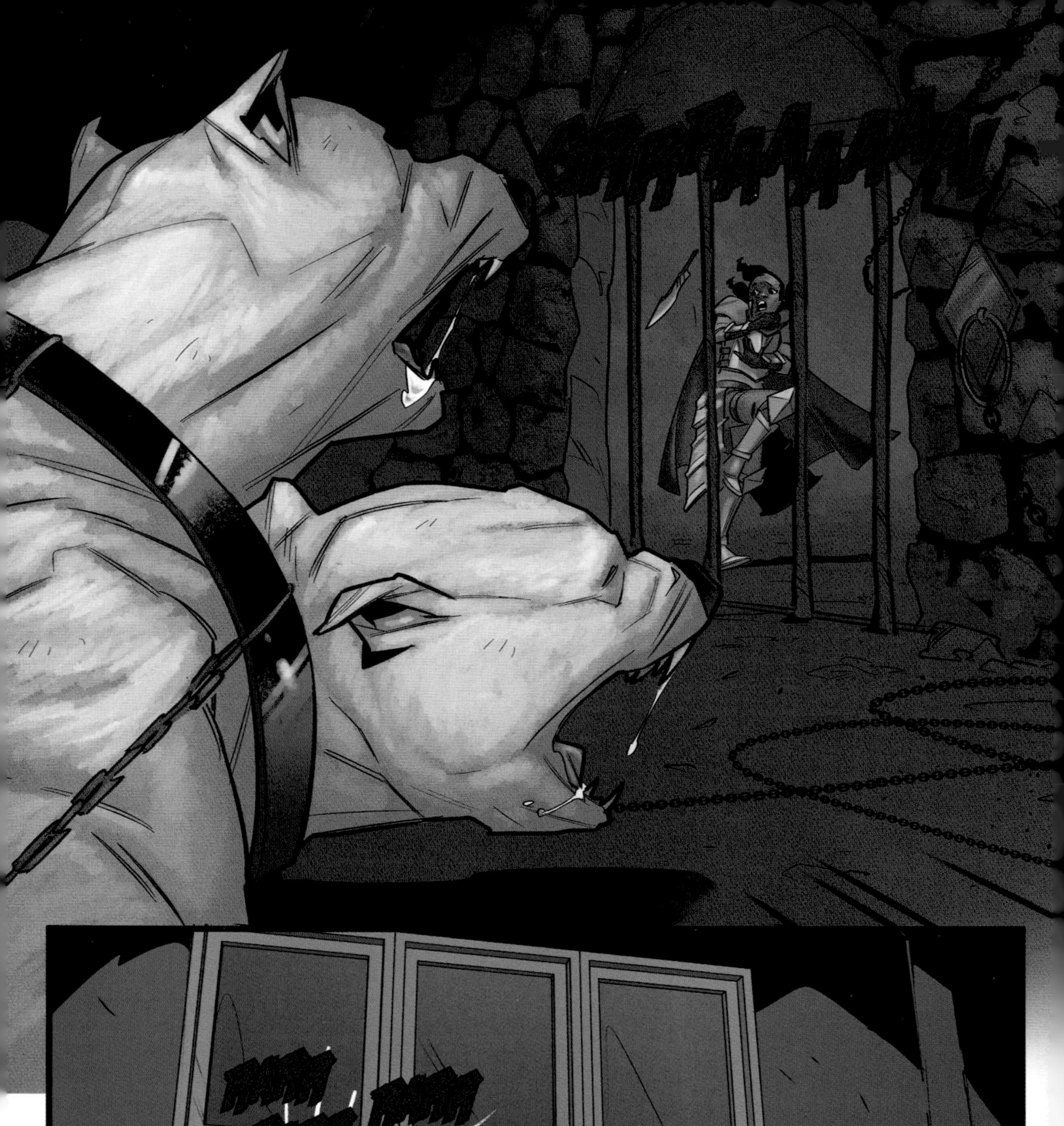
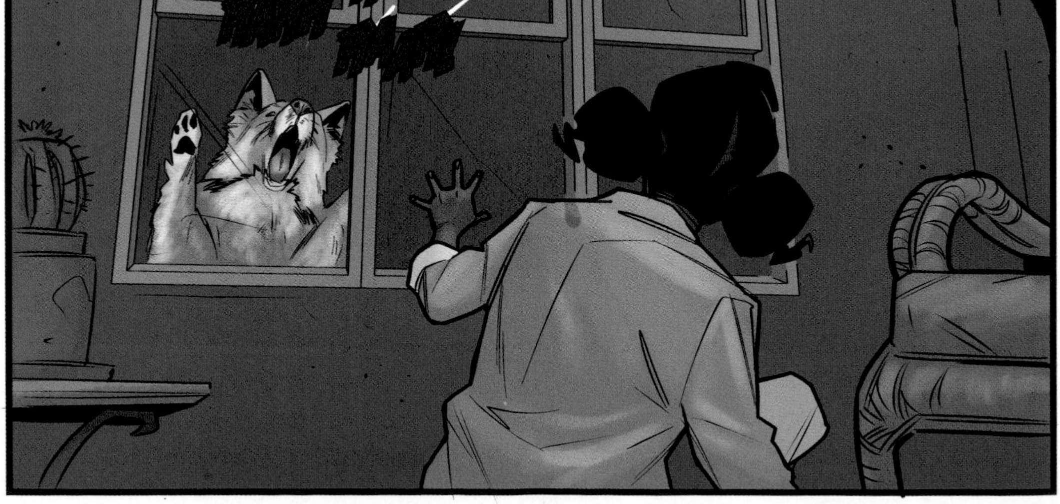

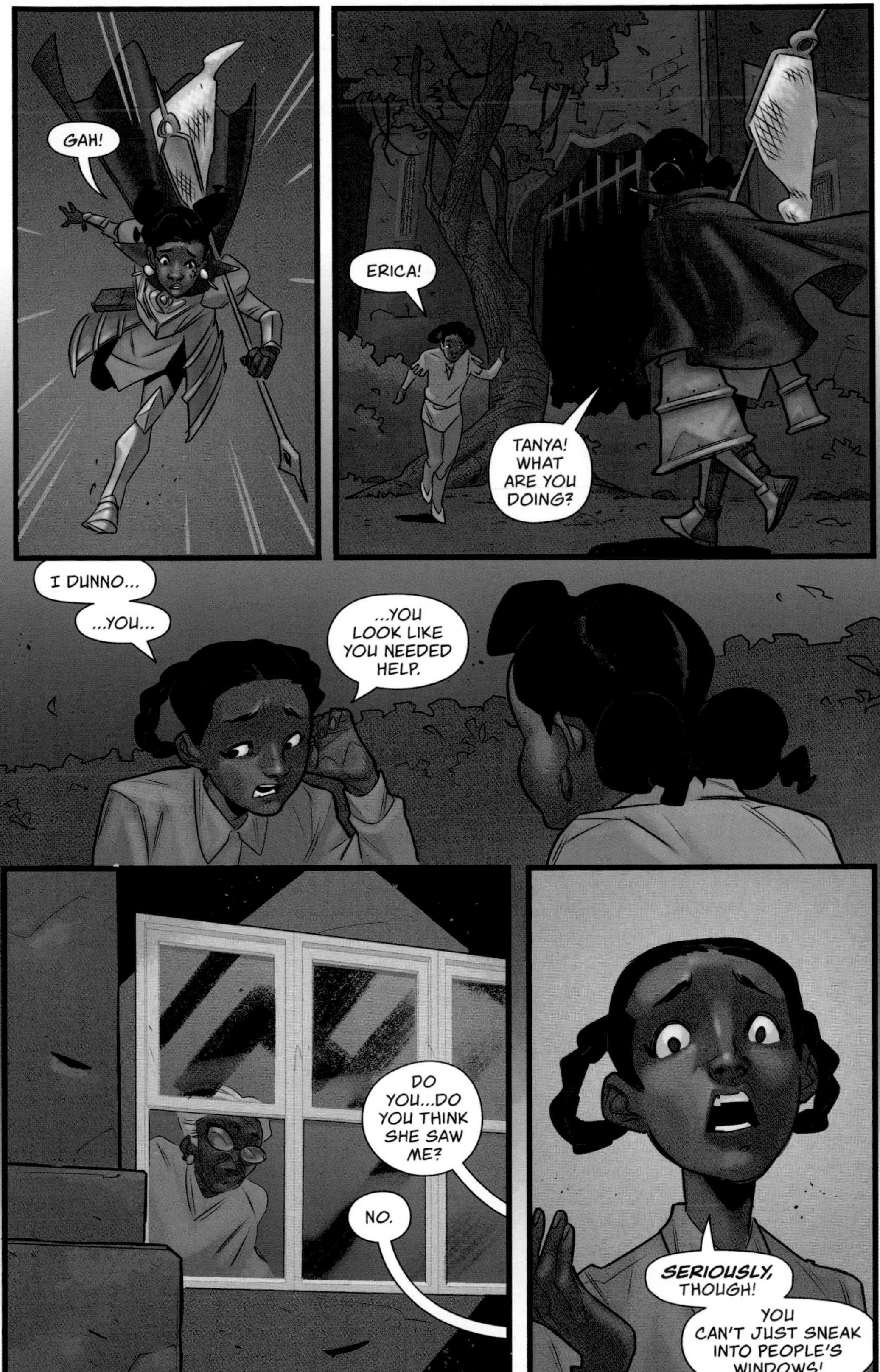
GAH!
ERICA!
TANYA! WHAT ARE YOU DOING?
I DUNNO...
...YOU...
...YOU LOOK LIKE YOU NEEDED HELP.
DO YOU...DO YOU THINK SHE SAW ME?
NO.
SERIOUSLY, THOUGH!
YOU CAN'T JUST SNEAK INTO PEOPLE'S WINDOWS!

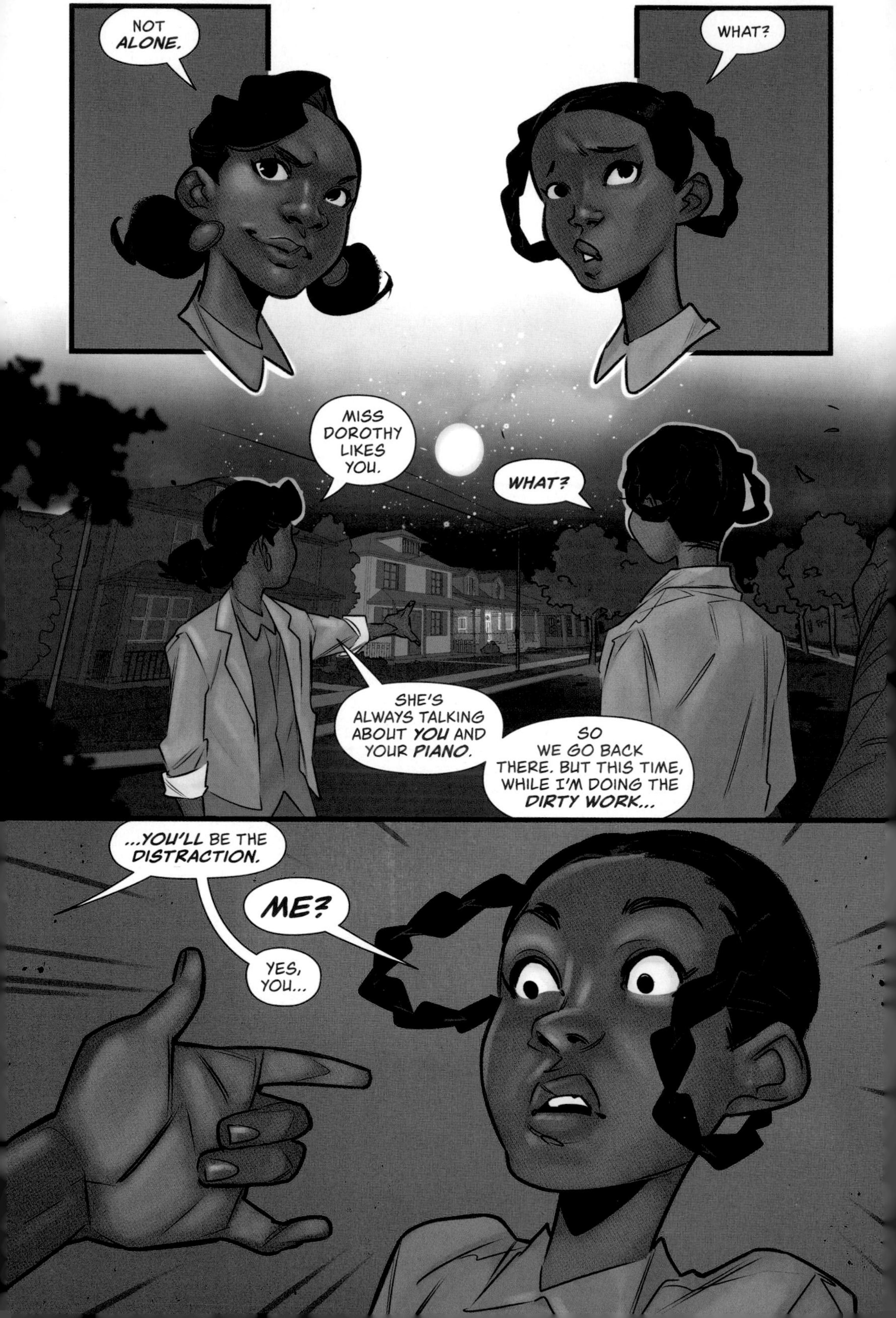
NOT ALONE.
WHAT?
MISS DOROTHY LIKES YOU.
WHAT?
SHE'S ALWAYS TALKING ABOUT YOU AND YOUR PIANO.
SO WE GO BACK THERE. BUT THIS TIME, WHILE I'M DOING THE DIRTY WORK...
...YOU'LL BE THE DISTRACTION.
ME?
YES, YOU...

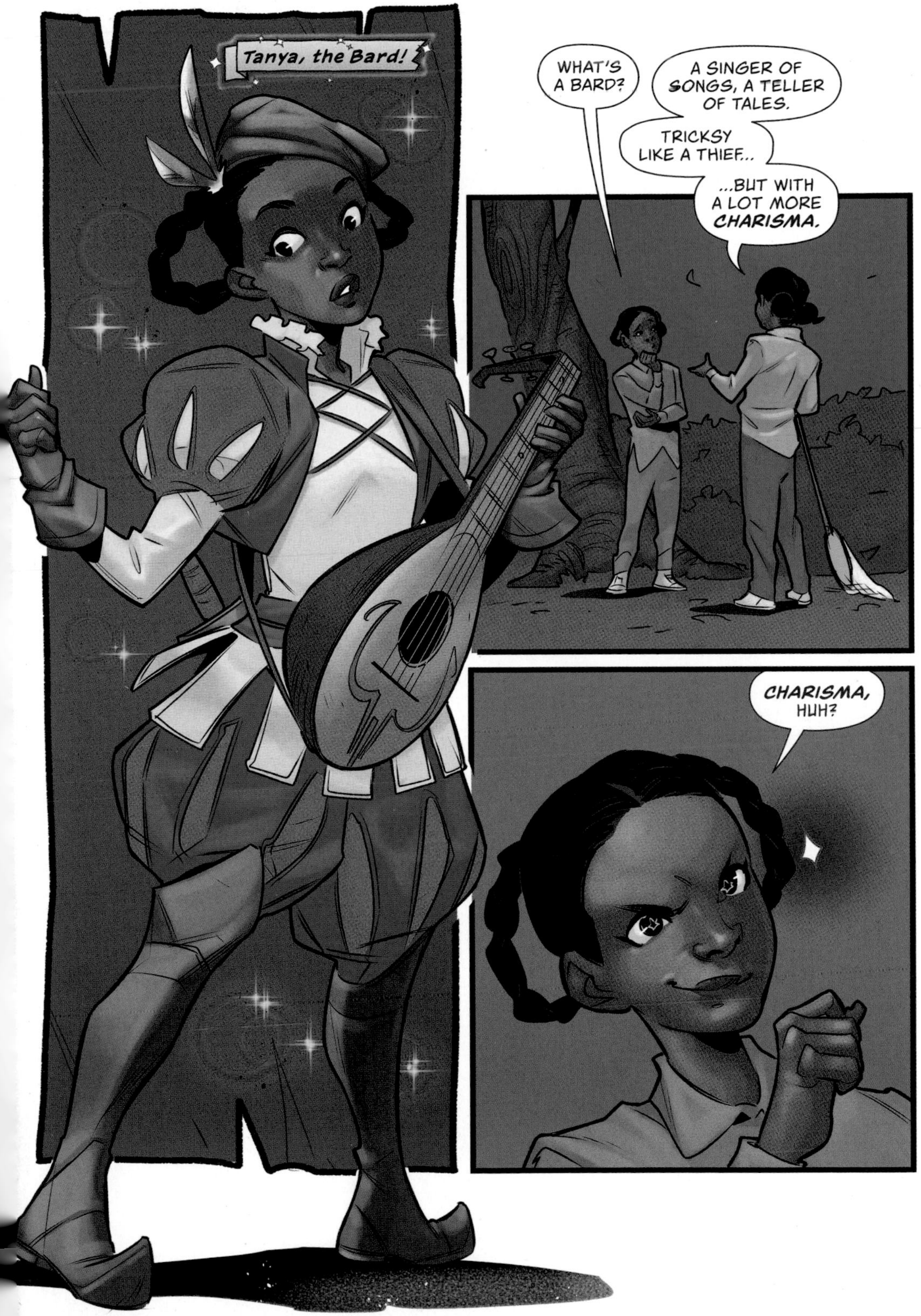
Tanya, the Bard!
WHAT'S A BARD?
A SINGER OF SONGS, A TELLER OF TALES.
TRICKSY LIKE A THIEF...
...BUT WITH A LOT MORE CHARISMA.
CHARISMA, HUH?

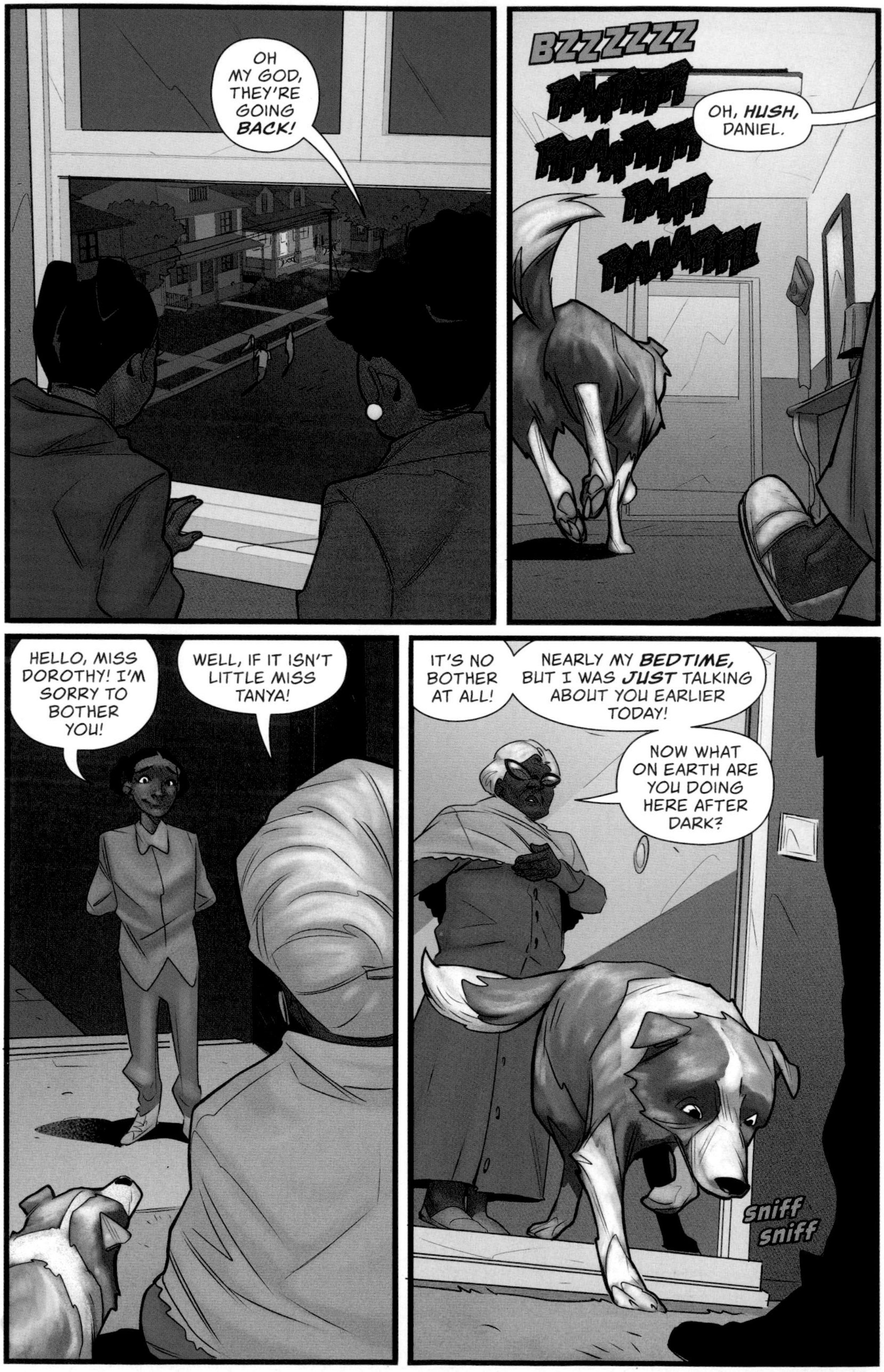
OH MY GOD, THEY'RE GOING **BACK**!
BZZZZZZ
OH, **HUSH**, DANIEL.
HELLO, MISS DOROTHY! I'M SORRY TO BOTHER YOU!
WELL, IF IT ISN'T LITTLE MISS TANYA!
IT'S NO BOTHER AT ALL!
NEARLY MY **BEDTIME**, BUT I WAS **JUST** TALKING ABOUT YOU EARLIER TODAY!
NOW WHAT ON EARTH ARE YOU DOING HERE AFTER DARK?
sniff sniff

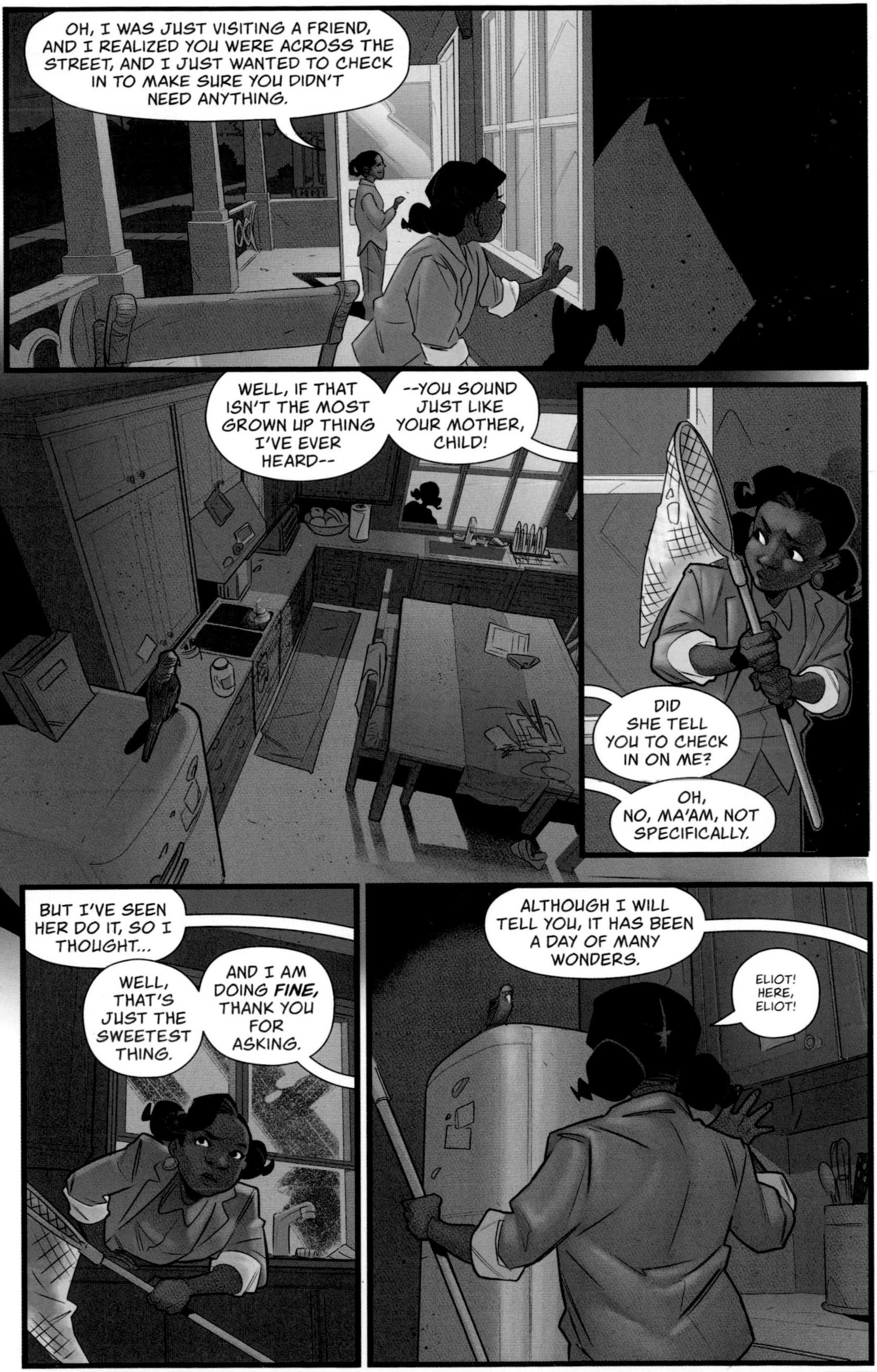
OH, I WAS JUST VISITING A FRIEND, AND I REALIZED YOU WERE ACROSS THE STREET, AND I JUST WANTED TO CHECK IN TO MAKE SURE YOU DIDN'T NEED ANYTHING.
WELL, IF THAT ISN'T THE MOST GROWN UP THING I'VE EVER HEARD--
--YOU SOUND JUST LIKE YOUR MOTHER, CHILD!
DID SHE TELL YOU TO CHECK IN ON ME?
OH, NO, MA'AM, NOT SPECIFICALLY.
BUT I'VE SEEN HER DO IT, SO I THOUGHT...
WELL, THAT'S JUST THE SWEETEST THING.
AND I AM DOING FINE, THANK YOU FOR ASKING.
ALTHOUGH I WILL TELL YOU, IT HAS BEEN A DAY OF MANY WONDERS.
ELIOT! HERE, ELIOT!

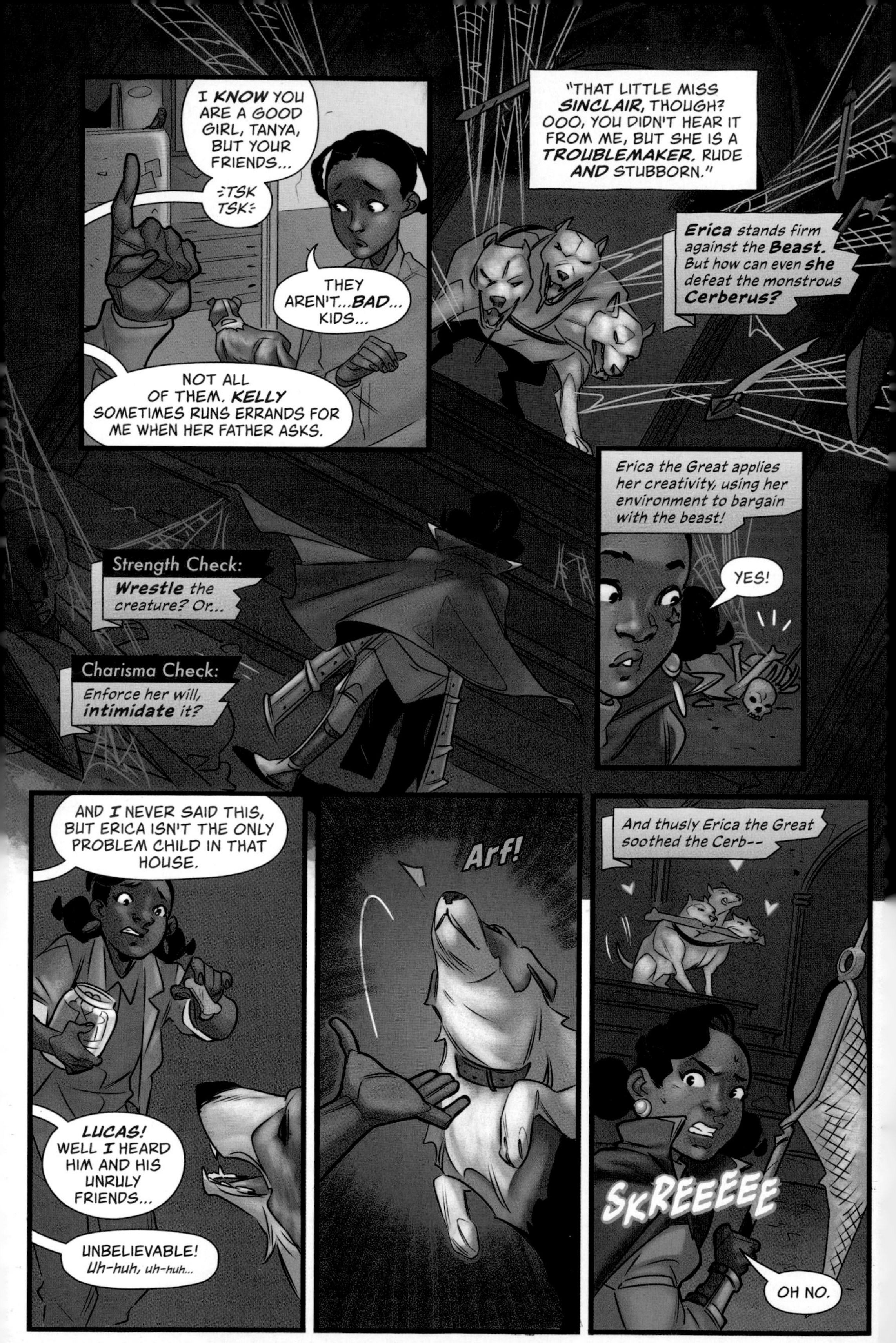
I KNOW YOU ARE A GOOD GIRL, TANYA, BUT YOUR FRIENDS...
TSK TSK
THEY AREN'T...BAD... KIDS...
NOT ALL OF THEM. KELLY SOMETIMES RUNS ERRANDS FOR ME WHEN HER FATHER ASKS.
"THAT LITTLE MISS SINCLAIR, THOUGH? OOO, YOU DIDN'T HEAR IT FROM ME, BUT SHE IS A TROUBLEMAKER. RUDE AND STUBBORN."
Erica stands firm against the Beast. But how can even she defeat the monstrous Cerberus?
Strength Check:
Wrestle the creature? Or...
Charisma Check:
Enforce her will, intimidate it?
Erica the Great applies her creativity, using her environment to bargain with the beast!
YES!
AND I NEVER SAID THIS, BUT ERICA ISN'T THE ONLY PROBLEM CHILD IN THAT HOUSE.
LUCAS! WELL I HEARD HIM AND HIS UNRULY FRIENDS...
UNBELIEVABLE! Uh-huh, uh-huh...
Arf!
And thusly Erica the Great soothed the Cerb--
SKREEEEEE
OH NO.

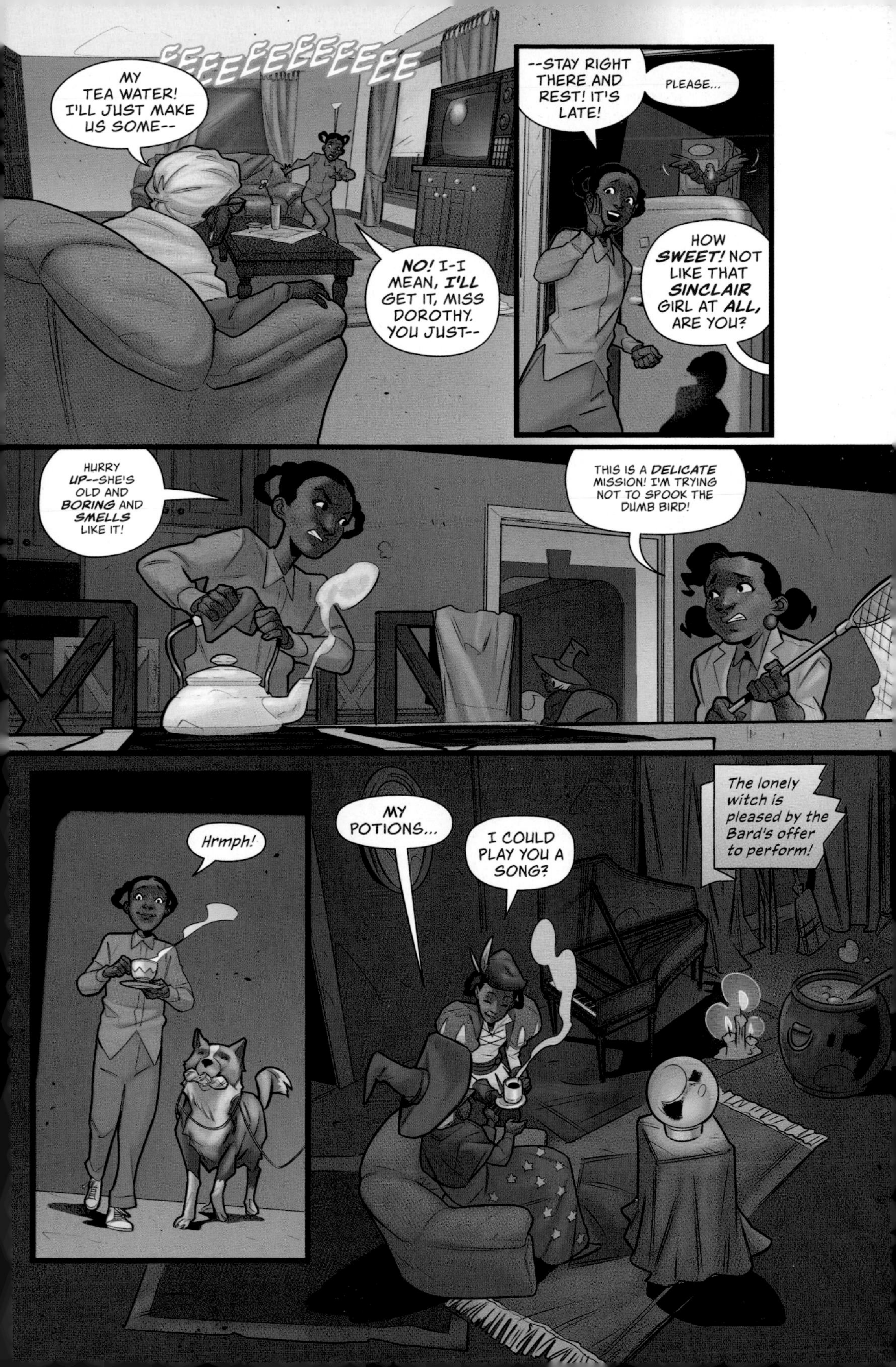
EEEEEEEEEEEEE
MY TEA WATER! I'LL JUST MAKE US SOME--
NO! I-I MEAN, I'LL GET IT, MISS DOROTHY. YOU JUST--
--STAY RIGHT THERE AND REST! IT'S LATE!
PLEASE...
HOW SWEET! NOT LIKE THAT SINCLAIR GIRL AT ALL, ARE YOU?
HURRY UP--SHE'S OLD AND BORING AND SMELLS LIKE IT!
THIS IS A DELICATE MISSION! I'M TRYING NOT TO SPOOK THE DUMB BIRD!
Hrmph!
MY POTIONS...
I COULD PLAY YOU A SONG?
The lonely witch is pleased by the Bard's offer to perform!

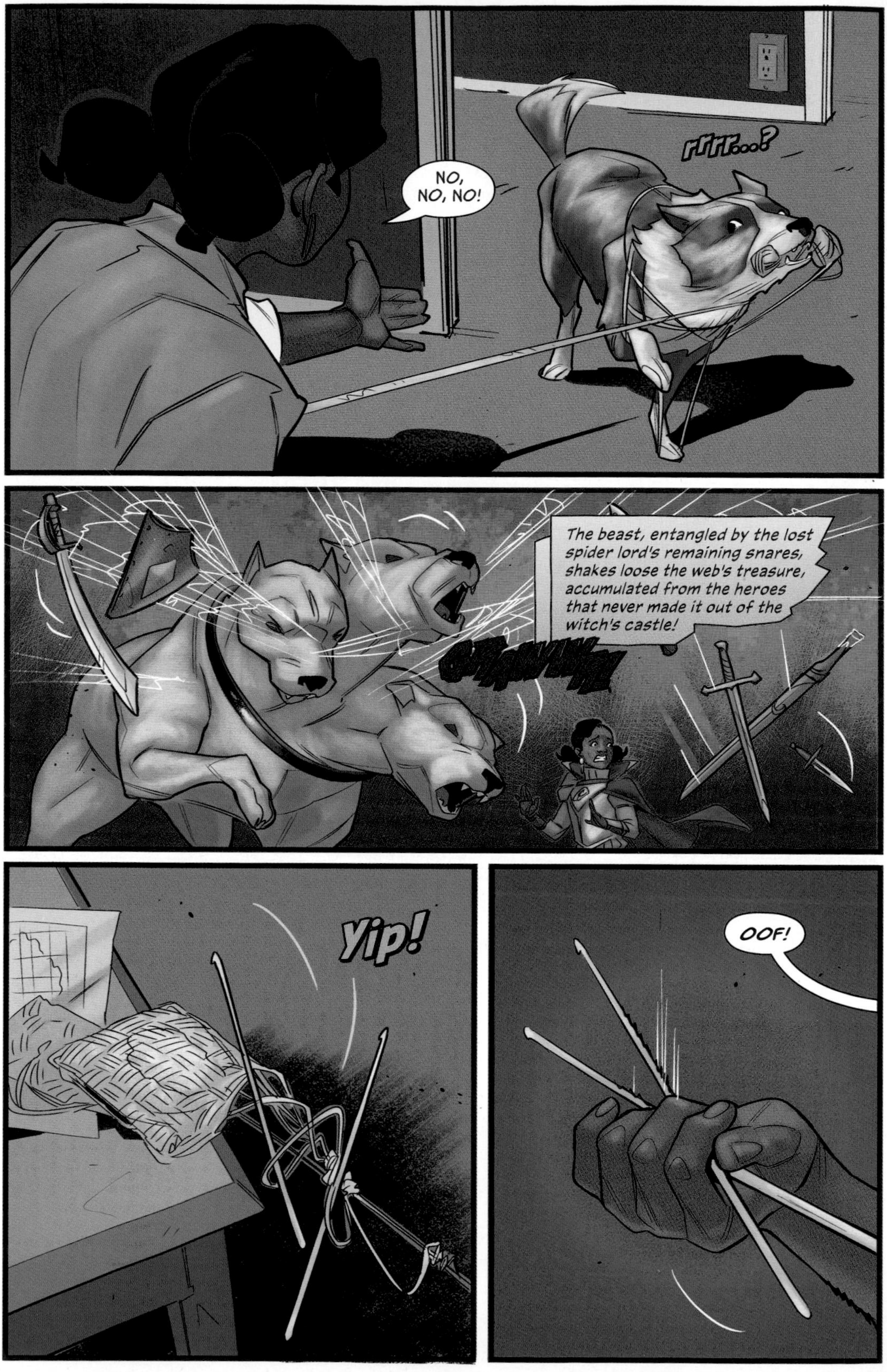
NO, NO, NO!
rrrr...?
The beast, entangled by the lost spider lord's remaining snares, shakes loose the web's treasure, accumulated from the heroes that never made it out of the witch's castle!
Yip!
OOF!

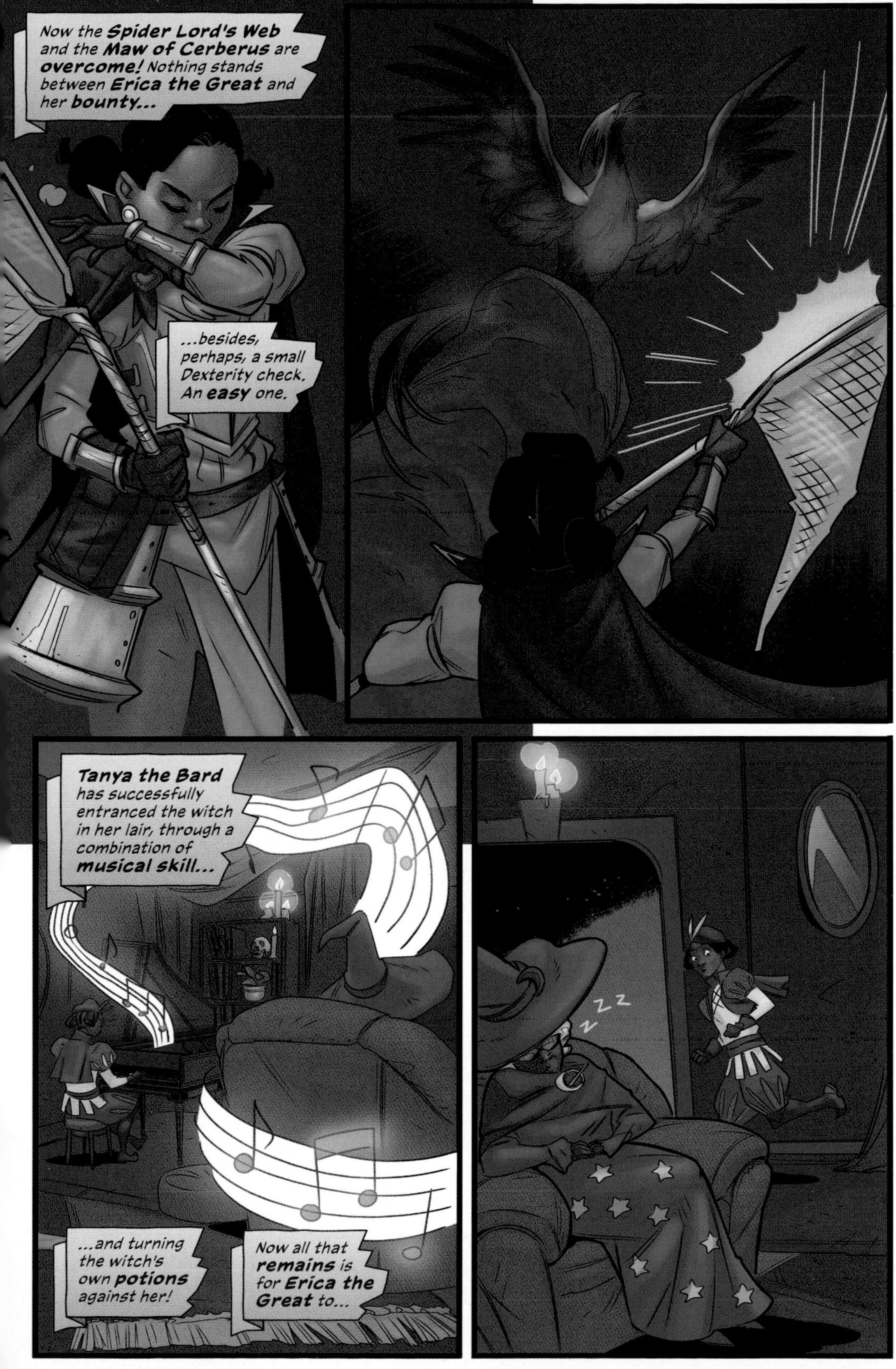
Now the Spider Lord's Web and the Maw of Cerberus are overcome! Nothing stands between Erica the Great and her bounty...
...besides, perhaps, a small Dexterity check. An easy one.
Tanya the Bard has successfully entranced the witch in her lair, through a combination of musical skill...
...and turning the witch's own potions against her!
Now all that remains is for Erica the Great to...
Z Z Z

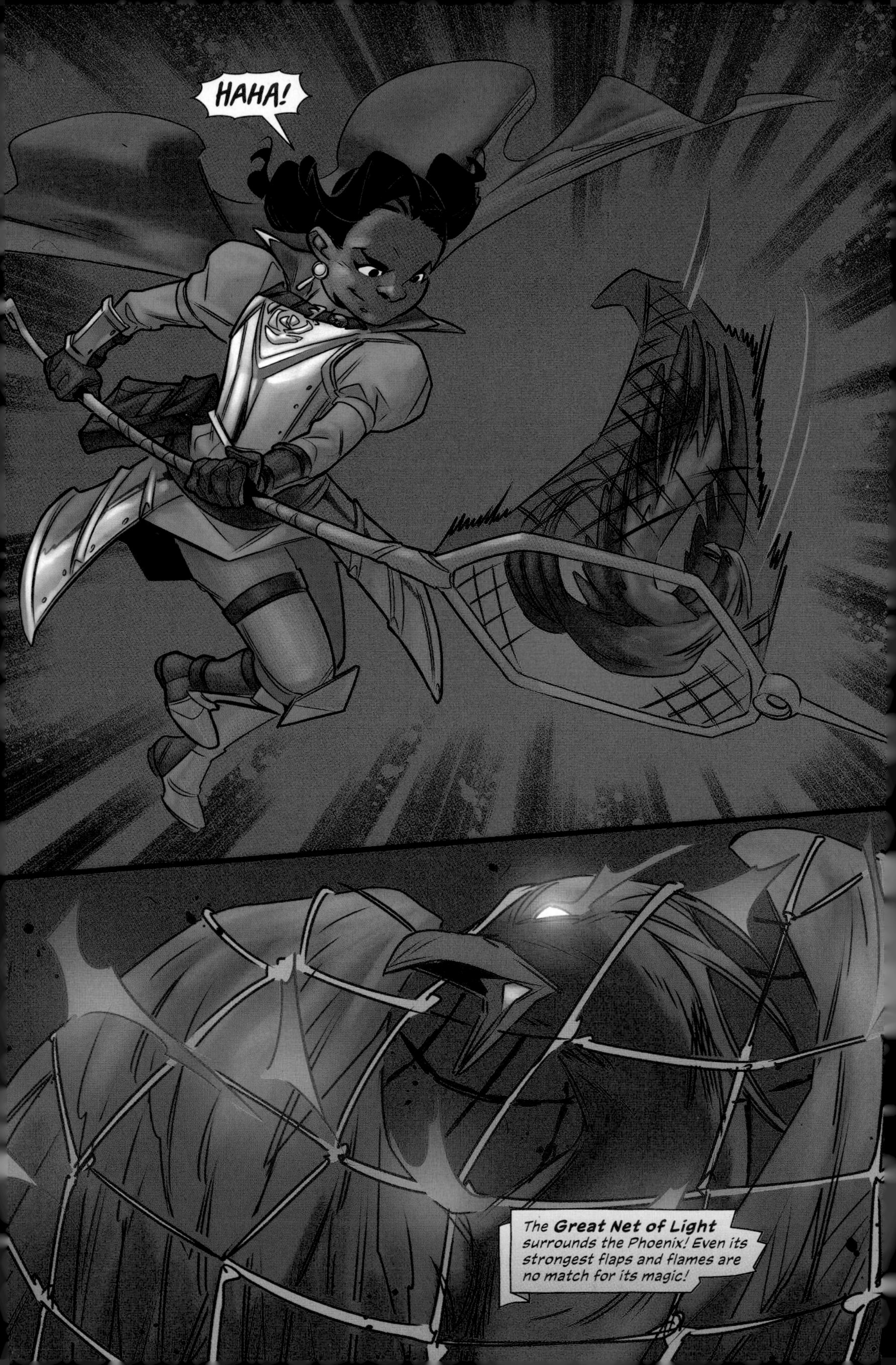
HAHA!
The **Great Net of Light** surrounds the Phoenix! Even its strongest flaps and flames are no match for its magic!

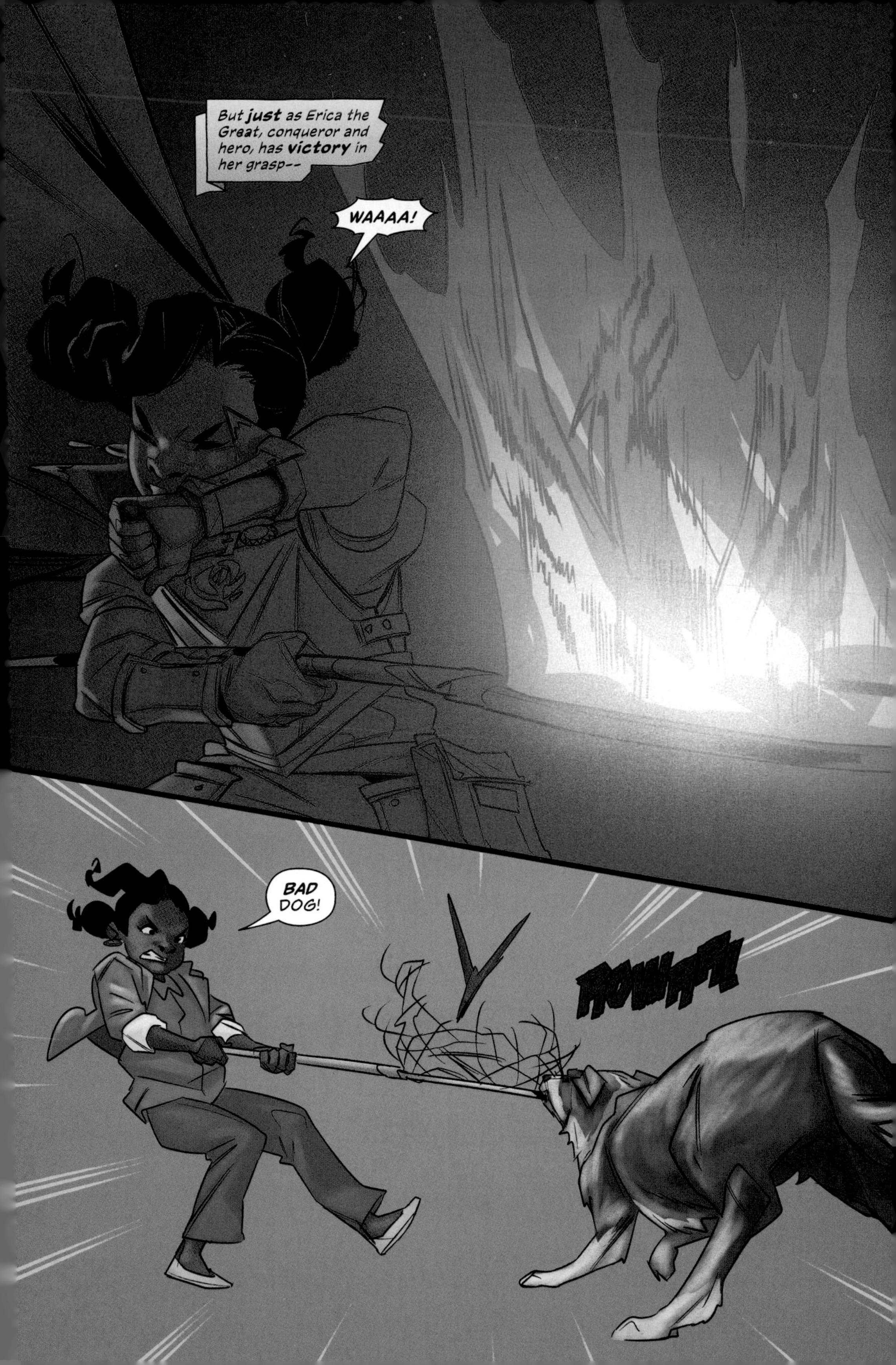
But just as Erica the Great, conqueror and hero, has victory in her grasp--
WAAAA!
BAD DOG!

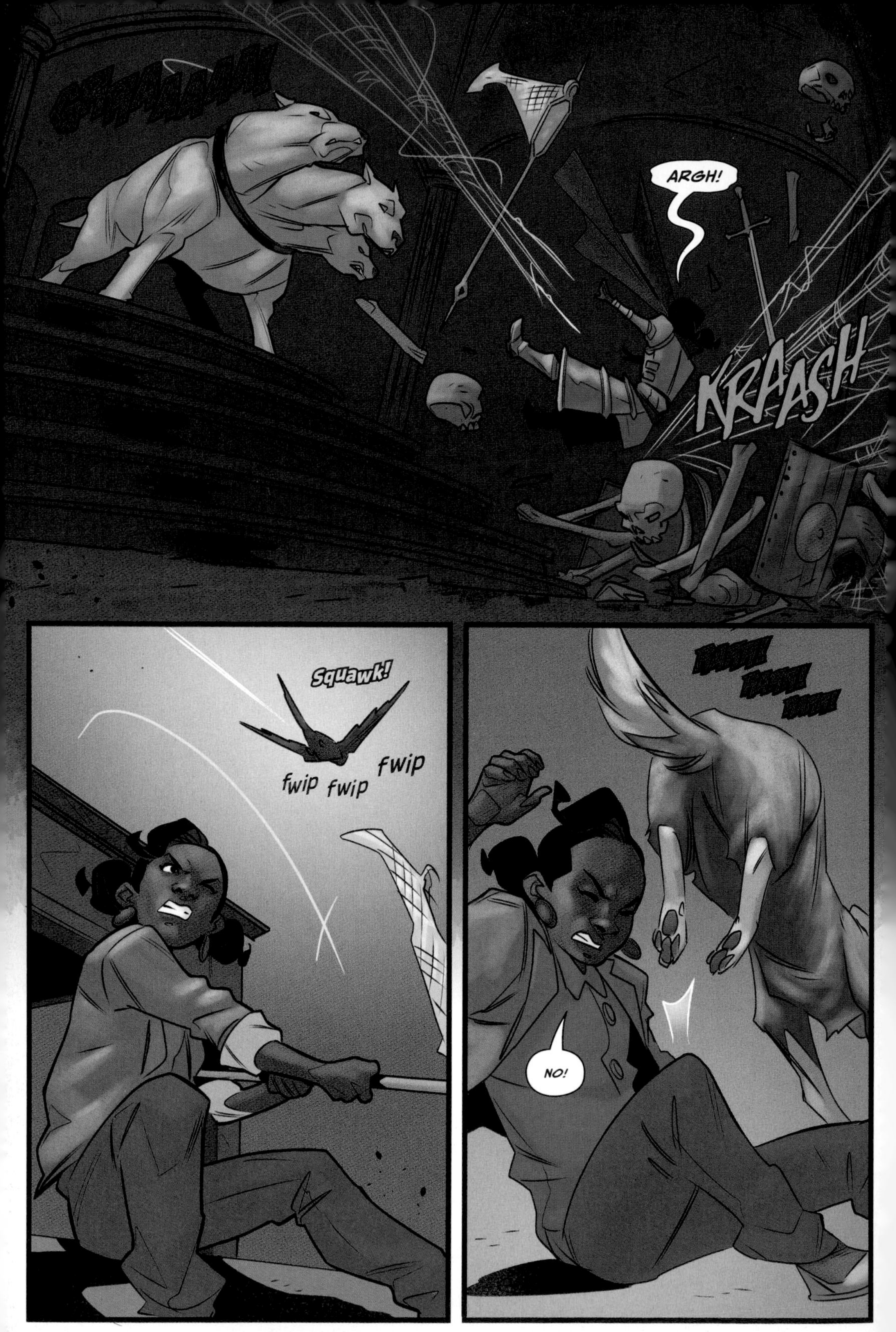
ARGH!
KRAASH
Squawk!
fwip fwip fwip
NO!

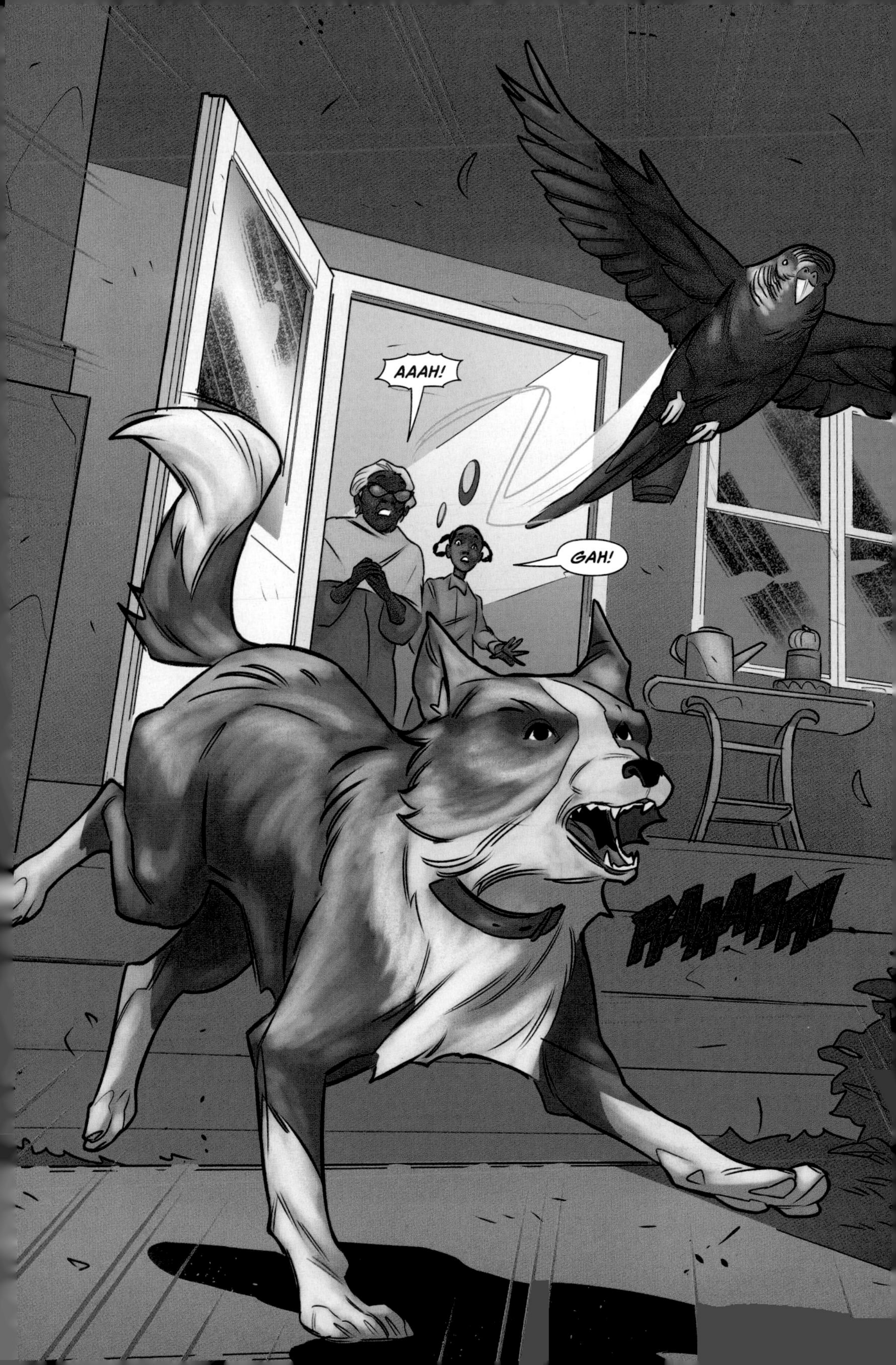
AAAH!
GAH!

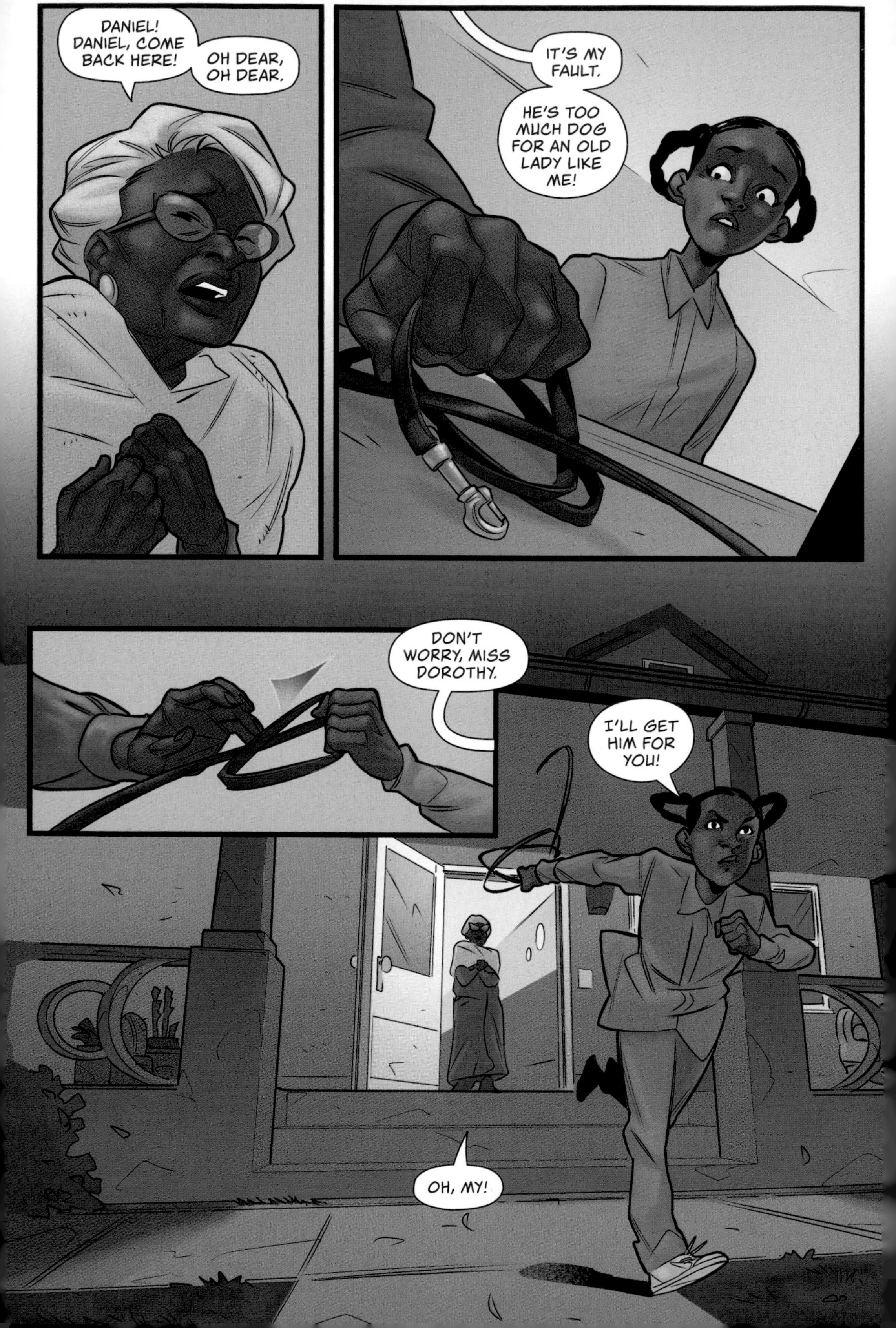
DANIEL! DANIEL, COME BACK HERE!
OH DEAR, OH DEAR.
IT'S MY FAULT.
HE'S TOO MUCH DOG FOR AN OLD LADY LIKE ME!
DON'T WORRY, MISS DOROTHY.
I'LL GET HIM FOR YOU!
OH, MY!

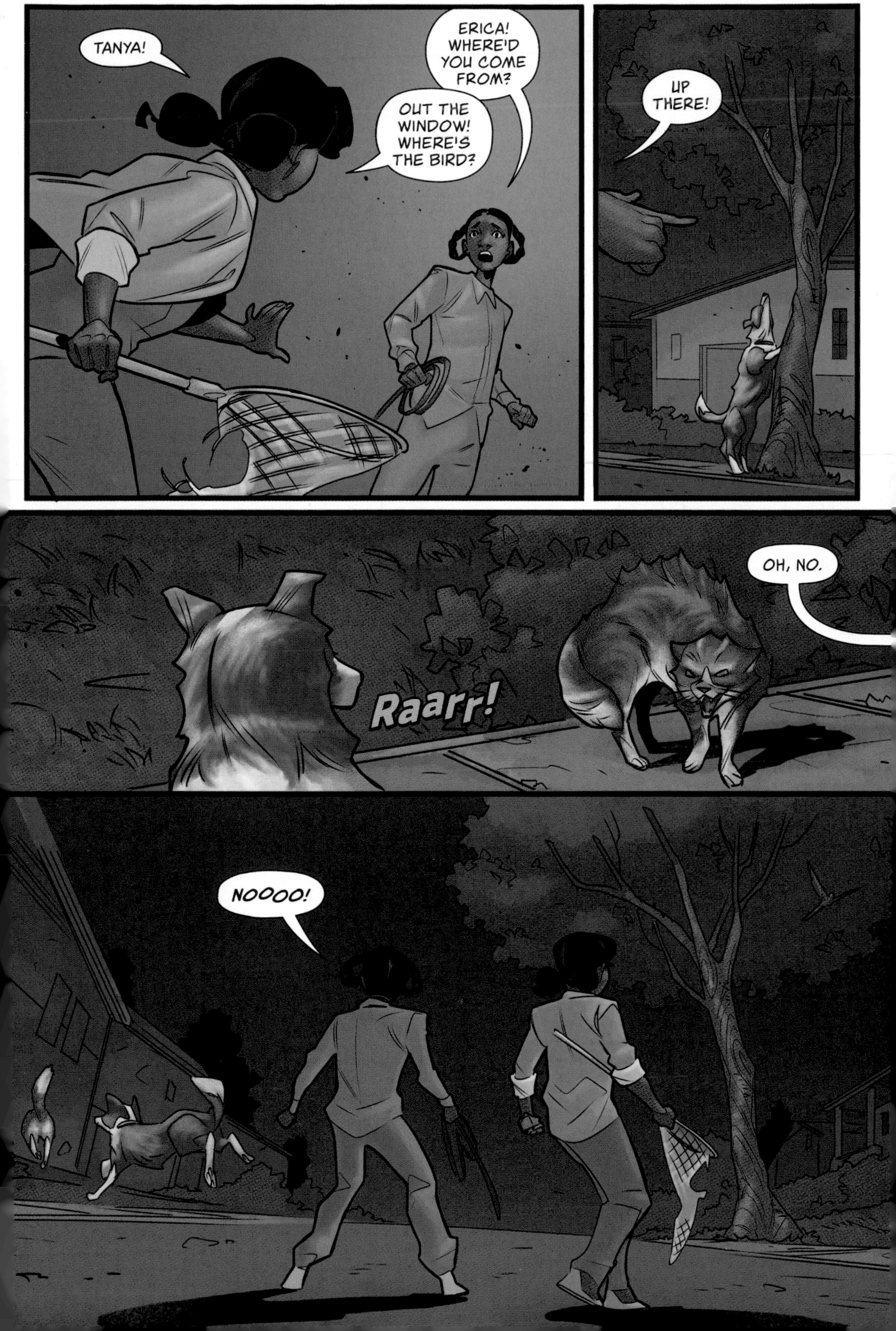
TANYA!
ERICA! WHERE'D YOU COME FROM?
OUT THE WINDOW! WHERE'S THE BIRD?
UP THERE!
Raarr!
OH, NO.
NOOOO!

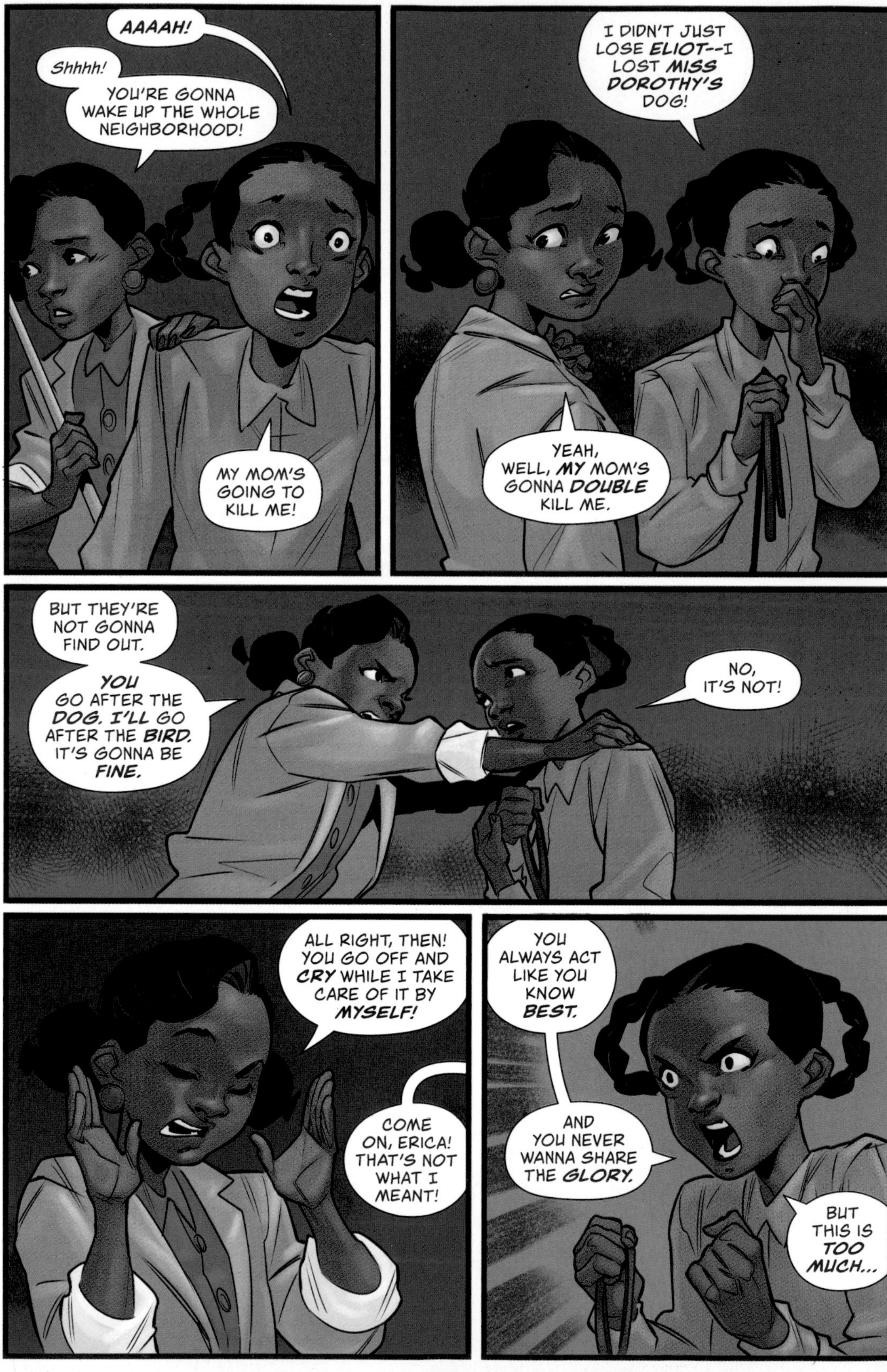
AAAAH!
Shhhh!
YOU'RE GONNA WAKE UP THE WHOLE NEIGHBORHOOD!
MY MOM'S GOING TO KILL ME!
I DIDN'T JUST LOSE ELIOT--I LOST MISS DOROTHY'S DOG!
YEAH, WELL, MY MOM'S GONNA DOUBLE KILL ME.
BUT THEY'RE NOT GONNA FIND OUT.
YOU GO AFTER THE DOG. I'LL GO AFTER THE BIRD. IT'S GONNA BE FINE.
NO, IT'S NOT!
ALL RIGHT, THEN! YOU GO OFF AND CRY WHILE I TAKE CARE OF IT BY MYSELF!
COME ON, ERICA! THAT'S NOT WHAT I MEANT!
YOU ALWAYS ACT LIKE YOU KNOW BEST.
AND YOU NEVER WANNA SHARE THE GLORY.
BUT THIS IS TOO MUCH...

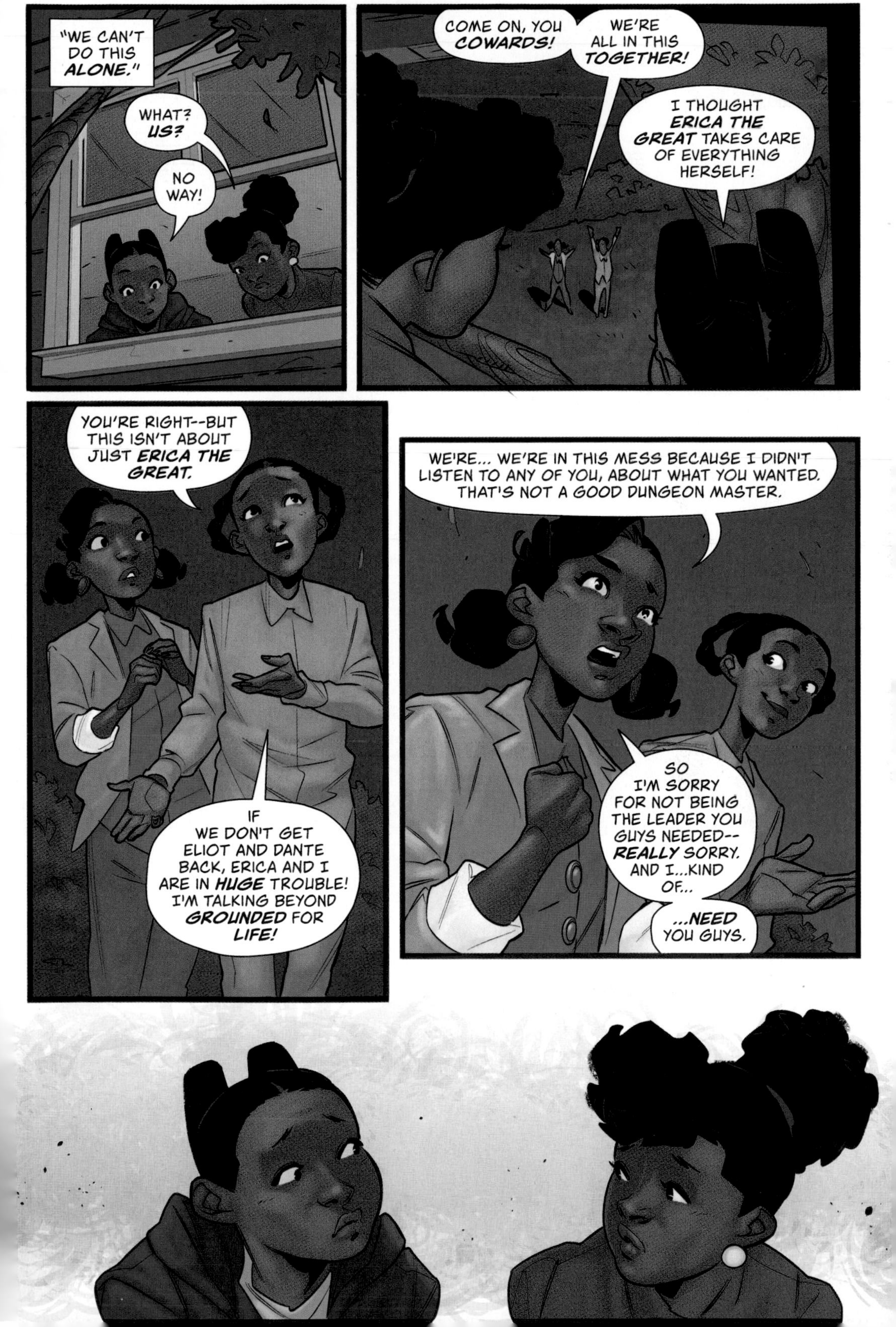
"WE CAN'T DO THIS ALONE."
WHAT? US?
NO WAY!
COME ON, YOU COWARDS!
WE'RE ALL IN THIS TOGETHER!
I THOUGHT ERICA THE GREAT TAKES CARE OF EVERYTHING HERSELF!
YOU'RE RIGHT--BUT THIS ISN'T ABOUT JUST ERICA THE GREAT.
IF WE DON'T GET ELIOT AND DANTE BACK, ERICA AND I ARE IN HUGE TROUBLE! I'M TALKING BEYOND GROUNDED FOR LIFE!
WE'RE... WE'RE IN THIS MESS BECAUSE I DIDN'T LISTEN TO ANY OF YOU, ABOUT WHAT YOU WANTED. THAT'S NOT A GOOD DUNGEON MASTER.
SO I'M SORRY FOR NOT BEING THE LEADER YOU GUYS NEEDED-- REALLY SORRY. AND I...KIND OF...
...NEED YOU GUYS.

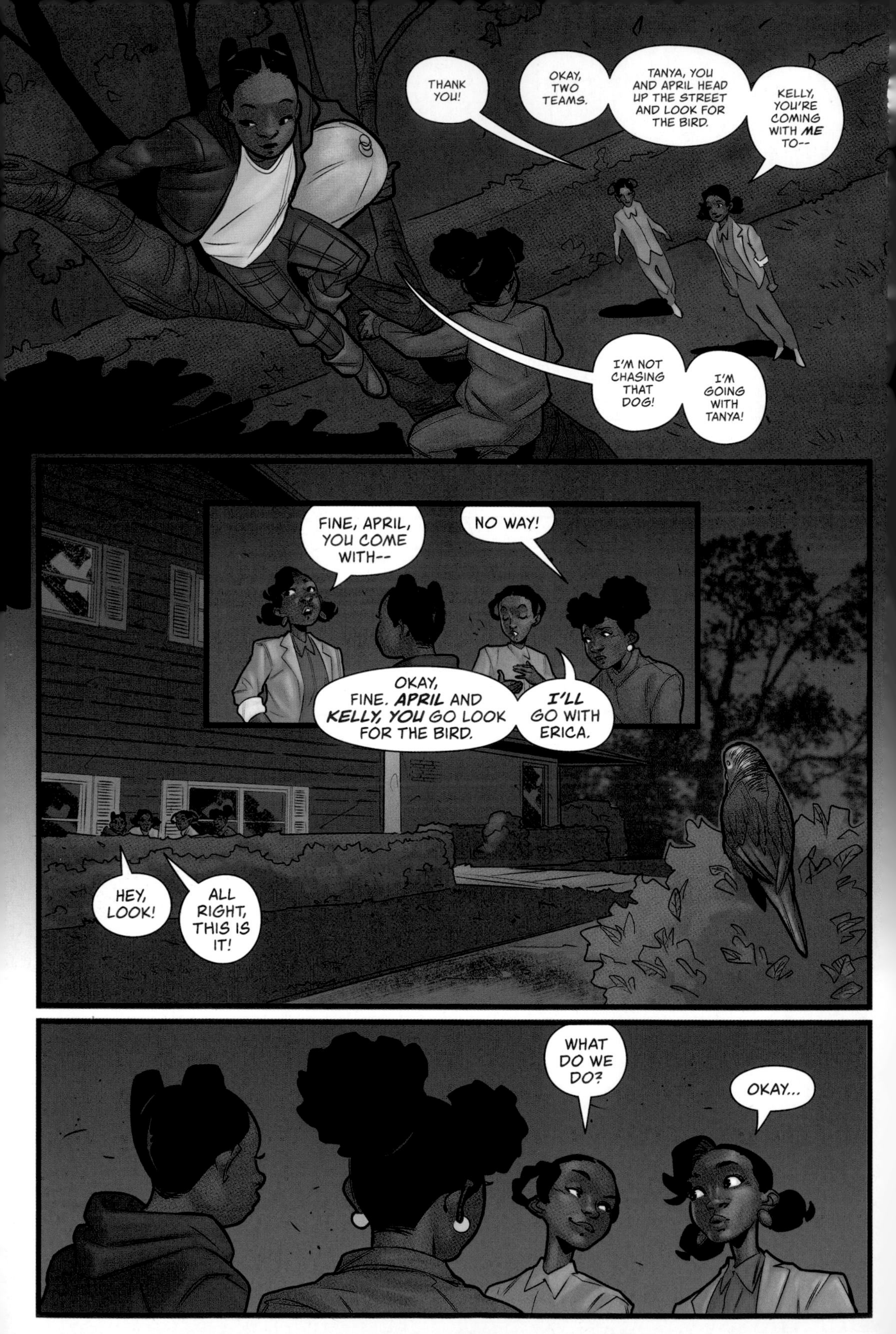
THANK YOU!
OKAY, TWO TEAMS.
TANYA, YOU AND APRIL HEAD UP THE STREET AND LOOK FOR THE BIRD.
KELLY, YOU'RE COMING WITH *ME* TO--
I'M NOT CHASING THAT DOG!
I'M GOING WITH TANYA!
FINE, APRIL, YOU COME WITH--
NO WAY!
OKAY, FINE. **APRIL** AND **KELLY, YOU** GO LOOK FOR THE BIRD.
I'LL GO WITH ERICA.
HEY, LOOK!
ALL RIGHT, THIS IS IT!
WHAT DO WE DO?
OKAY...

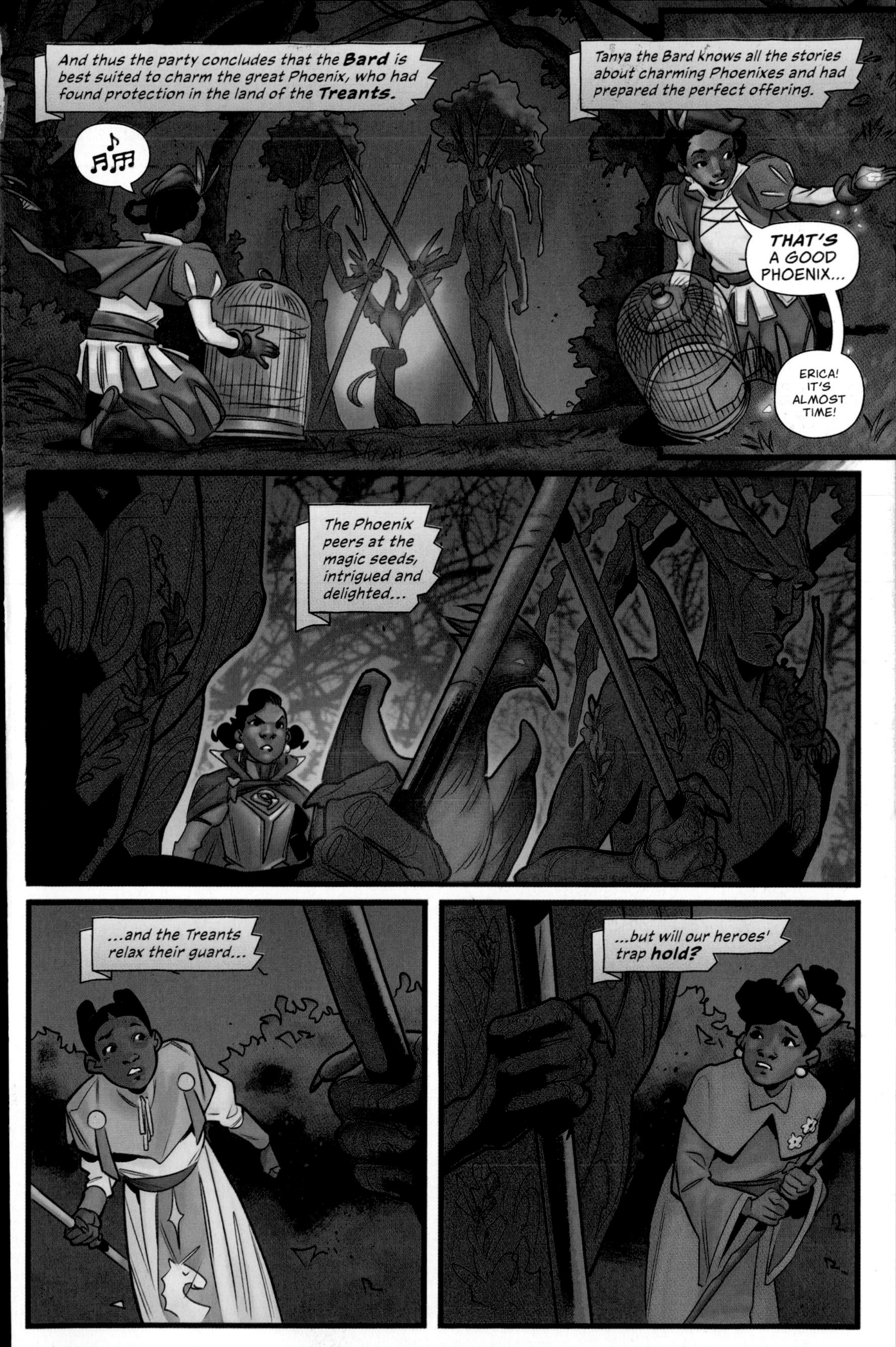
And thus the party concludes that the **Bard** is best suited to charm the great Phoenix, who had found protection in the land of the **Treants.**
Tanya the Bard knows all the stories about charming Phoenixes and had prepared the perfect offering.
THAT'S A GOOD PHOENIX...
ERICA! IT'S ALMOST TIME!
The Phoenix peers at the magic seeds, intrigued and delighted...
...and the Treants relax their guard...
...but will our heroes' trap **hold?**

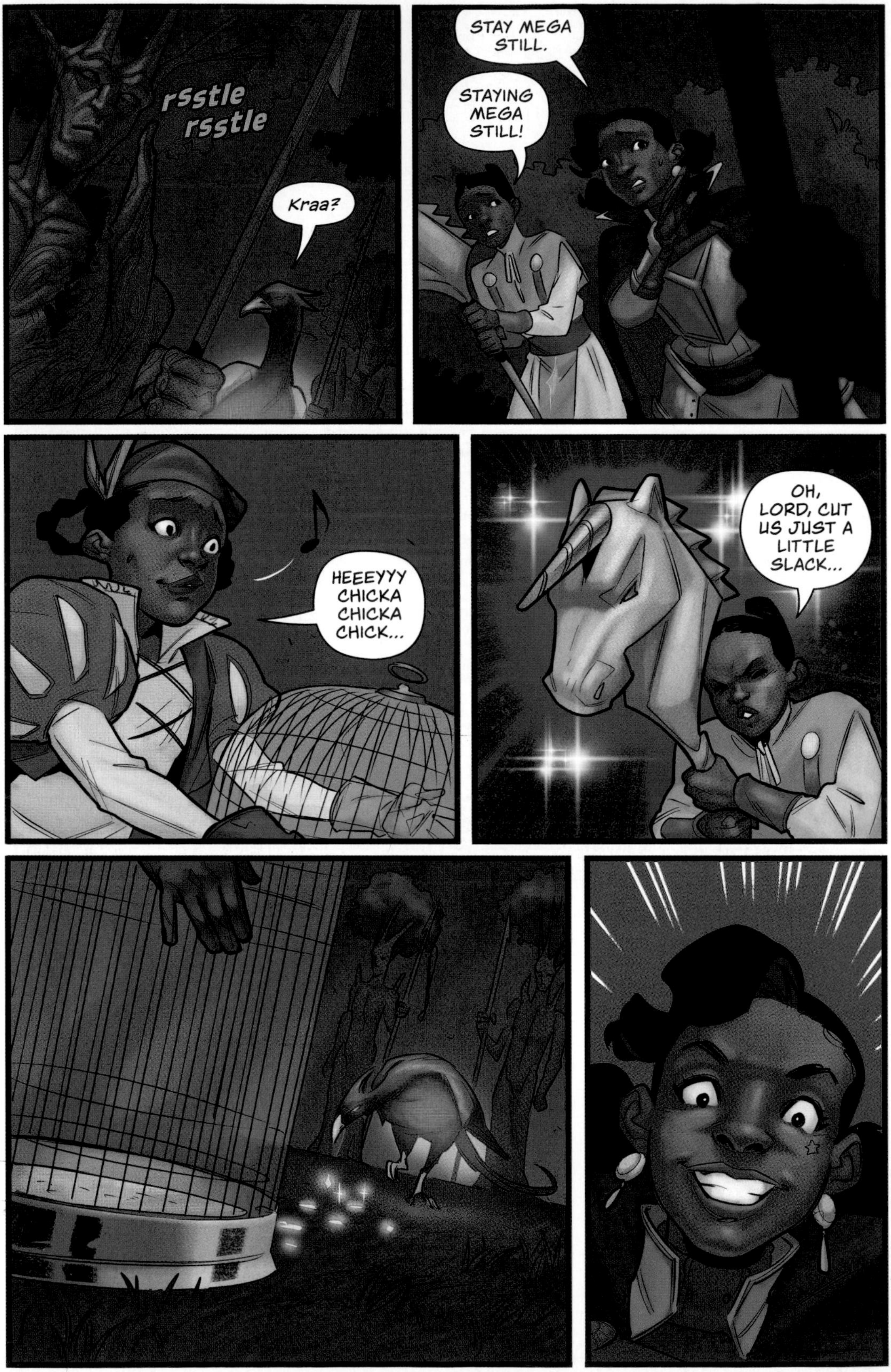
rsstle
rsstle
Kraa?
STAY MEGA STILL.
STAYING MEGA STILL!
HEEEYYY CHICKA CHICKA CHICK...
OH, LORD, CUT US JUST A LITTLE SLACK...

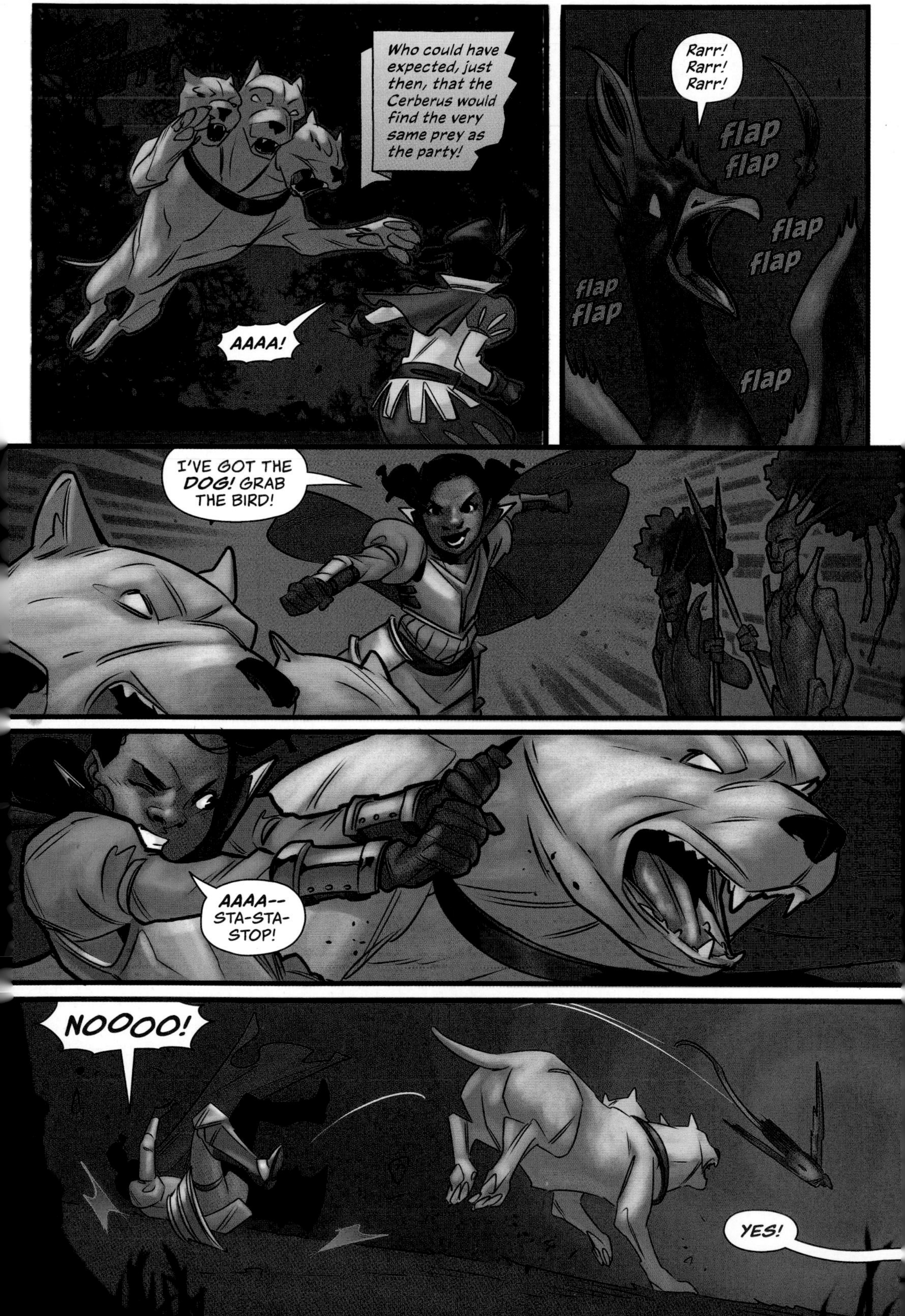

Who could have expected, just then, that the Cerberus would find the very same prey as the party!
AAAA!
Rarr! Rarr! Rarr!
flap flap
flap flap
flap flap
flap
I'VE GOT THE DOG! GRAB THE BIRD!
AAAA-- STA-STA-STOP!
NOOOO!
YES!

flap flap flap flap

ERICA! I GOT ELIOT!

THAT WAS *SO COOL* GUYS! I THOUGHT WE'D GET ALL SCRATCHED UP IN THE BUSHES!

Ha ha, ERICA, WHEN YOU GOT DRAGGED AROUND BY THAT BIG OL' DOG, YOU LOOKED RIDICULOUS!

YEAH, WELL...WE COULD HAVE SPENT TONIGHT DOING THIS BUT *COOLER* IN *DUNGEONS & DRAGONS,* YOU KNOW. THAT'S WHAT PARTIES *DO.*

AND IF *YOUR* GAME HAD THIS MUCH *TEAMWORK,* BET WE *WOULD* HAVE!

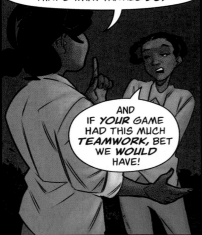

Ugh, WHATEVER. COME ON, WE STILL HAVE TO GET THAT *DOG.*

WAIT A MINUTE.

DO WE?

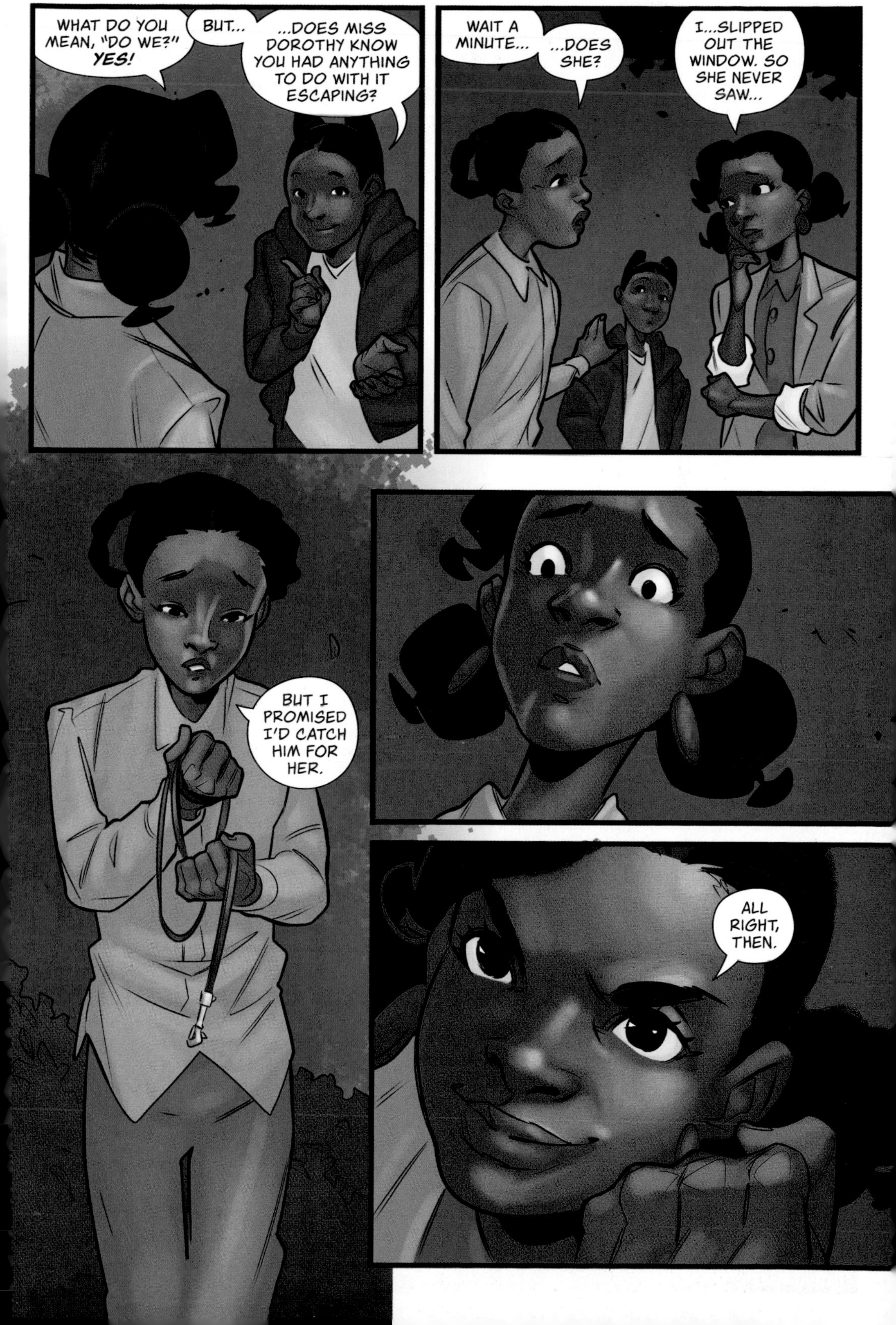

WHAT DO YOU MEAN, "DO WE?" YES!
BUT...
...DOES MISS DOROTHY KNOW YOU HAD ANYTHING TO DO WITH IT ESCAPING?
WAIT A MINUTE...
...DOES SHE?
I...SLIPPED OUT THE WINDOW. SO SHE NEVER SAW...
BUT I PROMISED I'D CATCH HIM FOR HER.
ALL RIGHT, THEN.

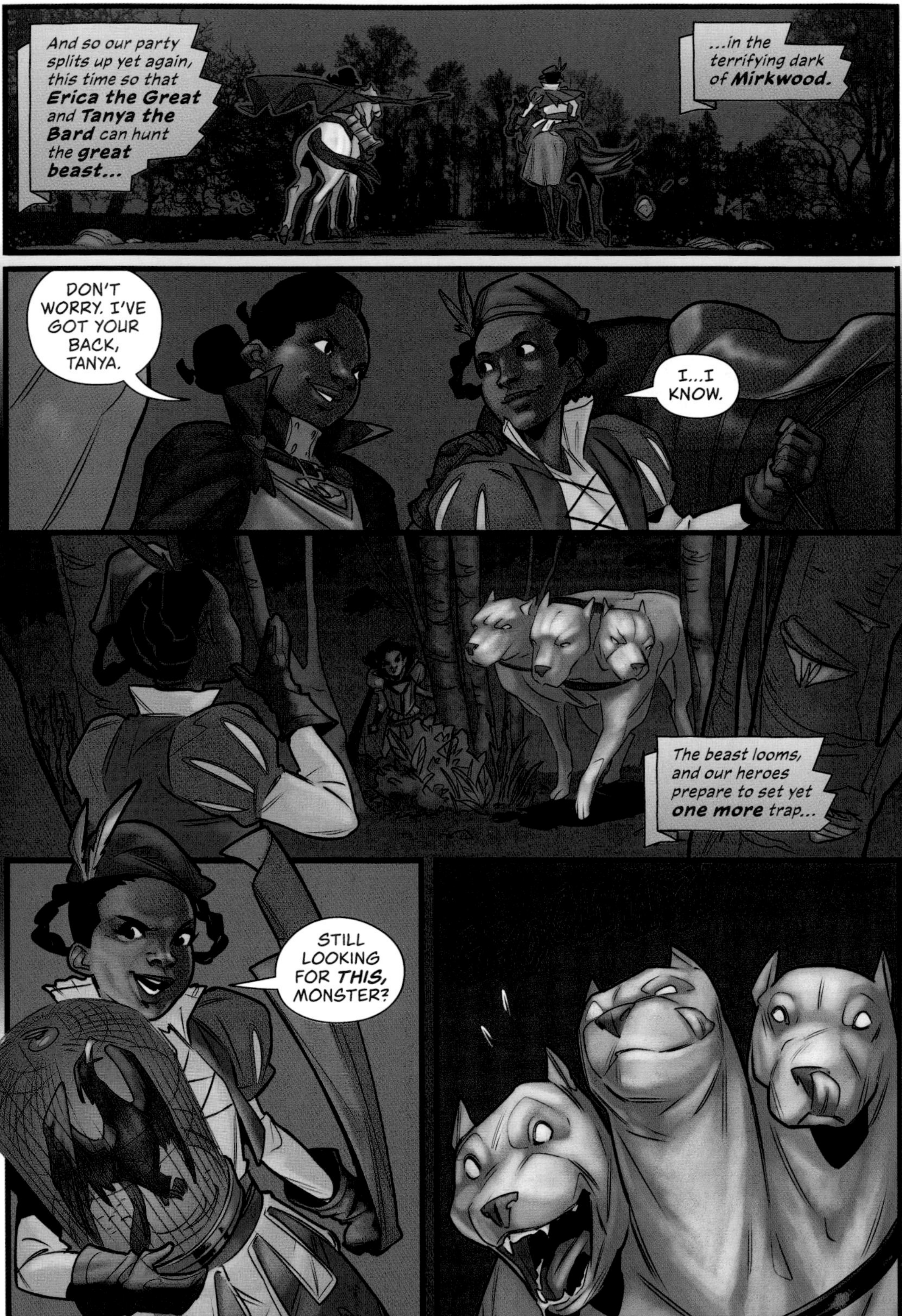
And so our party splits up yet again, this time so that **Erica the Great** and **Tanya the Bard** can hunt the **great beast...**
...in the terrifying dark of **Mirkwood.**
DON'T WORRY. I'VE GOT YOUR BACK, TANYA.
I...I KNOW.
The beast looms, and our heroes prepare to set yet **one more** trap...
STILL LOOKING FOR **THIS,** MONSTER?

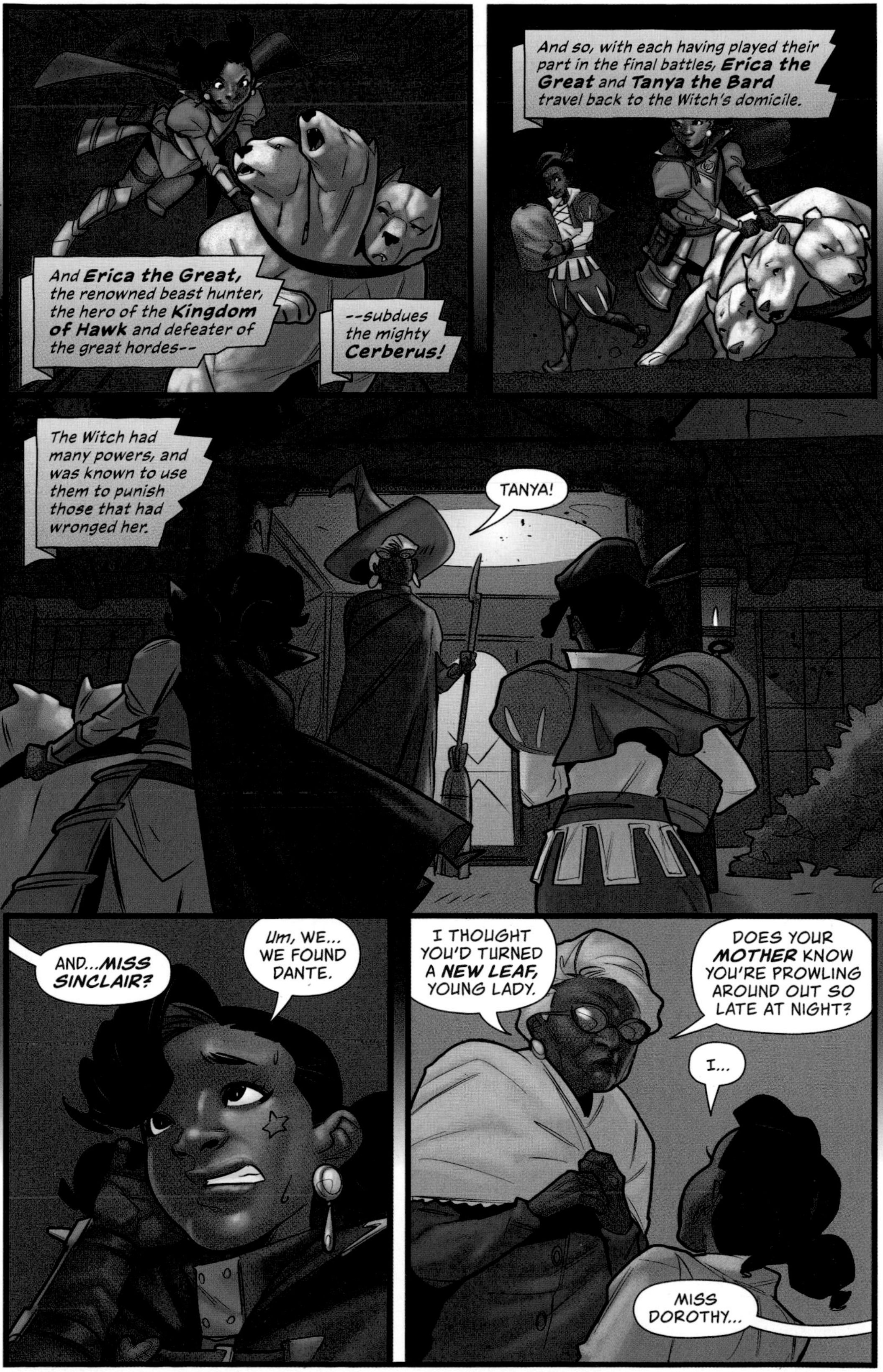
And **Erica the Great,** the renowned beast hunter, the hero of the **Kingdom of Hawk** and defeater of the great hordes--
--subdues the mighty **Cerberus!**
And so, with each having played their part in the final battles, **Erica the Great** and **Tanya the Bard** travel back to the Witch's domicile.
The Witch had many powers, and was known to use them to punish those that had wronged her.
TANYA!
AND...**MISS SINCLAIR?**
UM, WE... WE FOUND DANTE.
I THOUGHT YOU'D TURNED A **NEW LEAF,** YOUNG LADY.
DOES YOUR **MOTHER** KNOW YOU'RE PROWLING AROUND OUT SO LATE AT NIGHT?
I...
MISS DOROTHY...

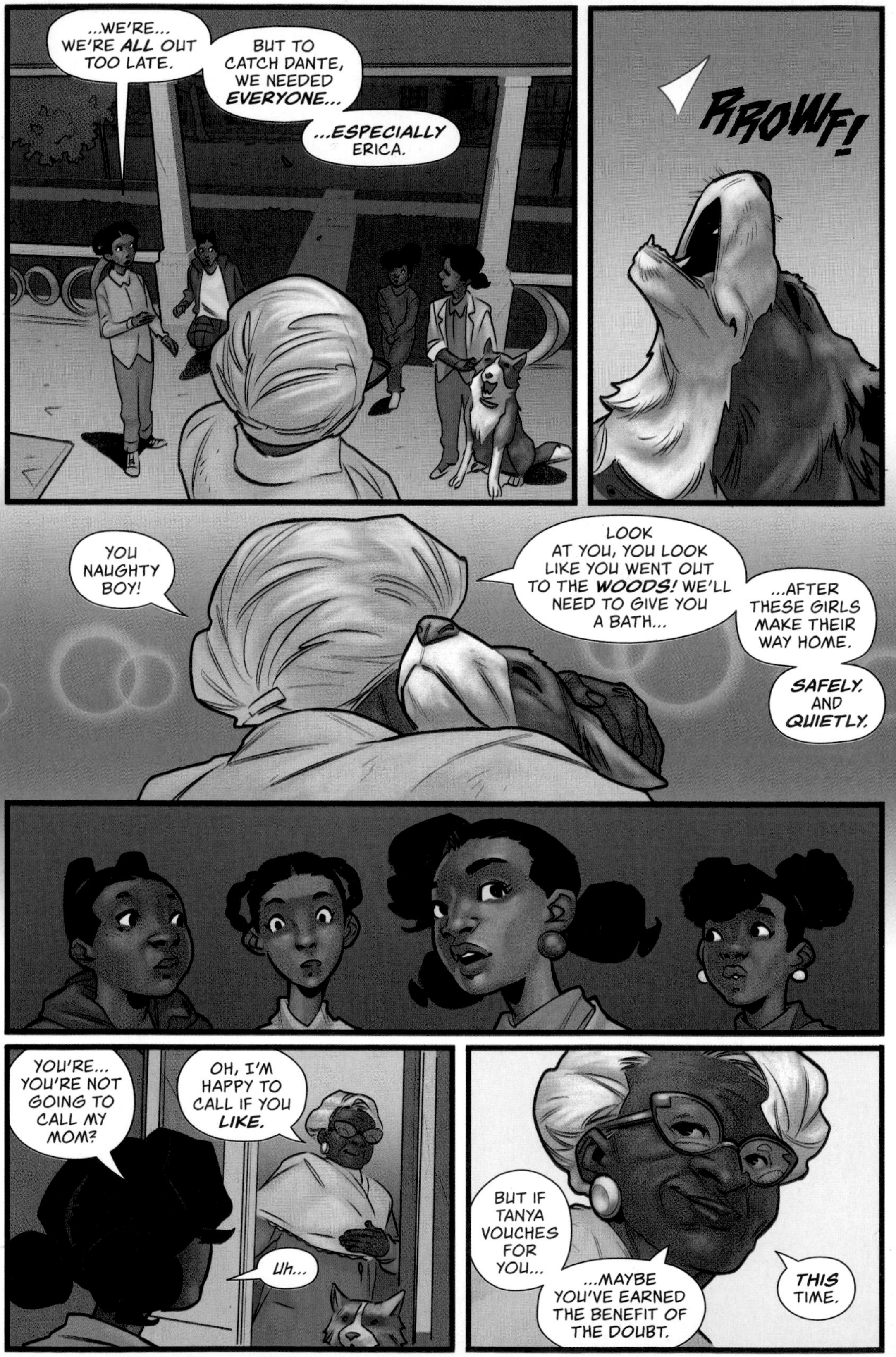
...WE'RE... WE'RE ALL OUT TOO LATE.
BUT TO CATCH DANTE, WE NEEDED EVERYONE...
...ESPECIALLY ERICA.
RROWF!
YOU NAUGHTY BOY!
LOOK AT YOU, YOU LOOK LIKE YOU WENT OUT TO THE WOODS! WE'LL NEED TO GIVE YOU A BATH...
...AFTER THESE GIRLS MAKE THEIR WAY HOME.
SAFELY. AND QUIETLY.
YOU'RE... YOU'RE NOT GOING TO CALL MY MOM?
OH, I'M HAPPY TO CALL IF YOU LIKE.
UH...
BUT IF TANYA VOUCHES FOR YOU...
...MAYBE YOU'VE EARNED THE BENEFIT OF THE DOUBT.
THIS TIME.

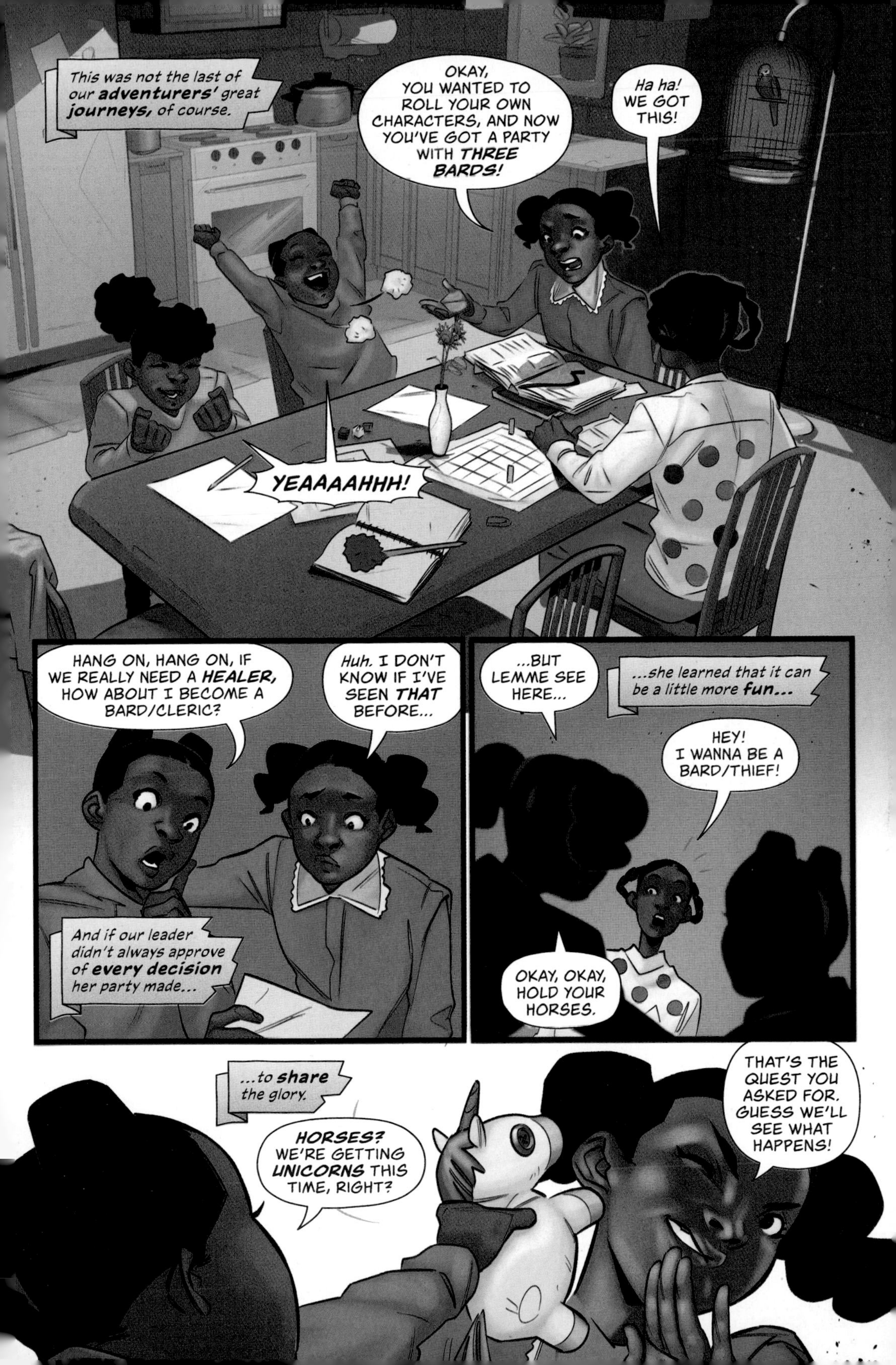
This was not the last of our adventurers' great journeys, of course.
OKAY, YOU WANTED TO ROLL YOUR OWN CHARACTERS, AND NOW YOU'VE GOT A PARTY WITH THREE BARDS!
Ha ha! WE GOT THIS!
YEAAAAHHH!
HANG ON, HANG ON, IF WE REALLY NEED A HEALER, HOW ABOUT I BECOME A BARD/CLERIC?
Huh. I DON'T KNOW IF I'VE SEEN THAT BEFORE...
And if our leader didn't always approve of every decision her party made...
...BUT LEMME SEE HERE...
...she learned that it can be a little more fun...
HEY! I WANNA BE A BARD/THIEF!
OKAY, OKAY, HOLD YOUR HORSES.
...to share the glory.
HORSES? WE'RE GETTING UNICORNS THIS TIME, RIGHT?
THAT'S THE QUEST YOU ASKED FOR. GUESS WE'LL SEE WHAT HAPPENS!

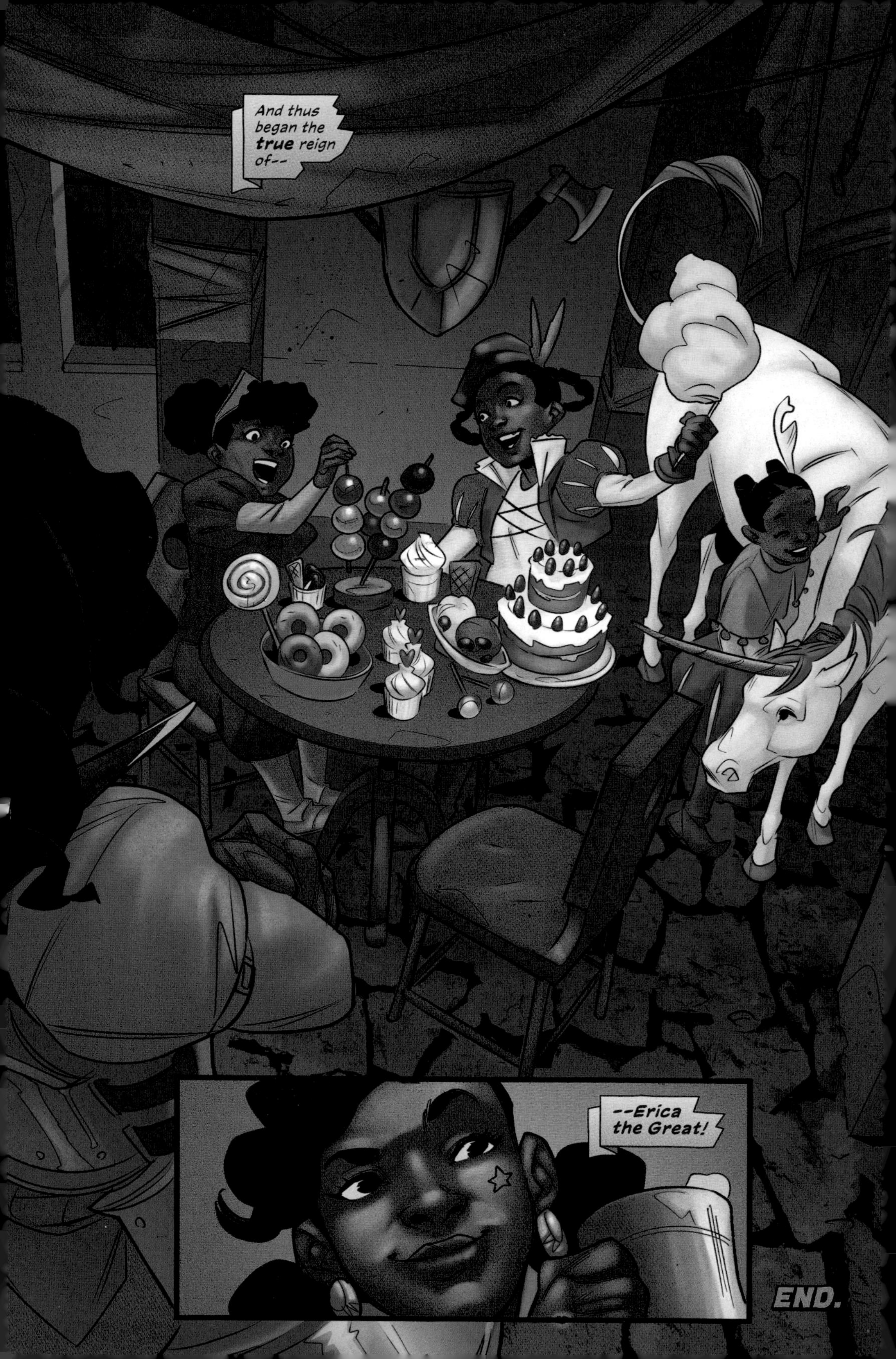
And thus began the true reign of--
--Erica the Great!
END.

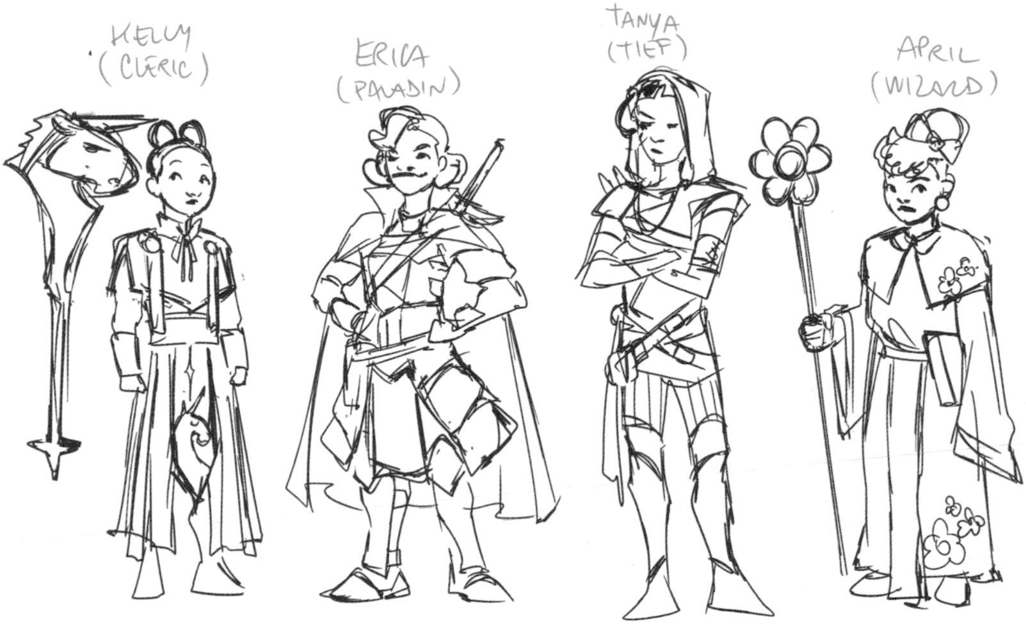
KELLY
(CLERIC)
ERICA
(PALADIN)
TANYA
(TIEF)
APRIL
(WIZARD)

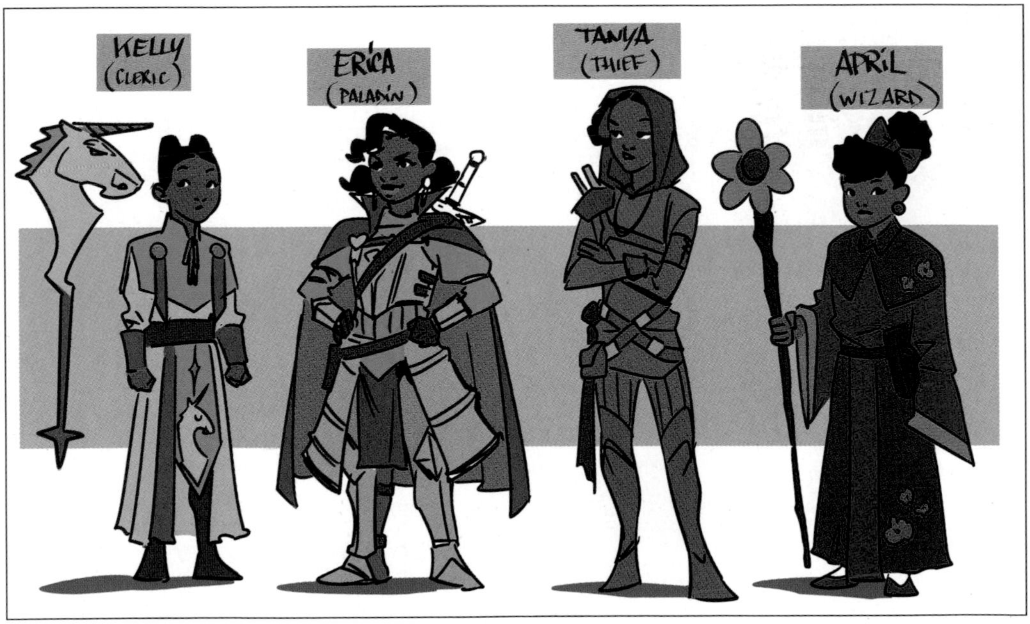
KELLY
(CLERIC)
ERICA
(PALADIN)
TANYA
(THIEF)
APRIL
(WIZARD)

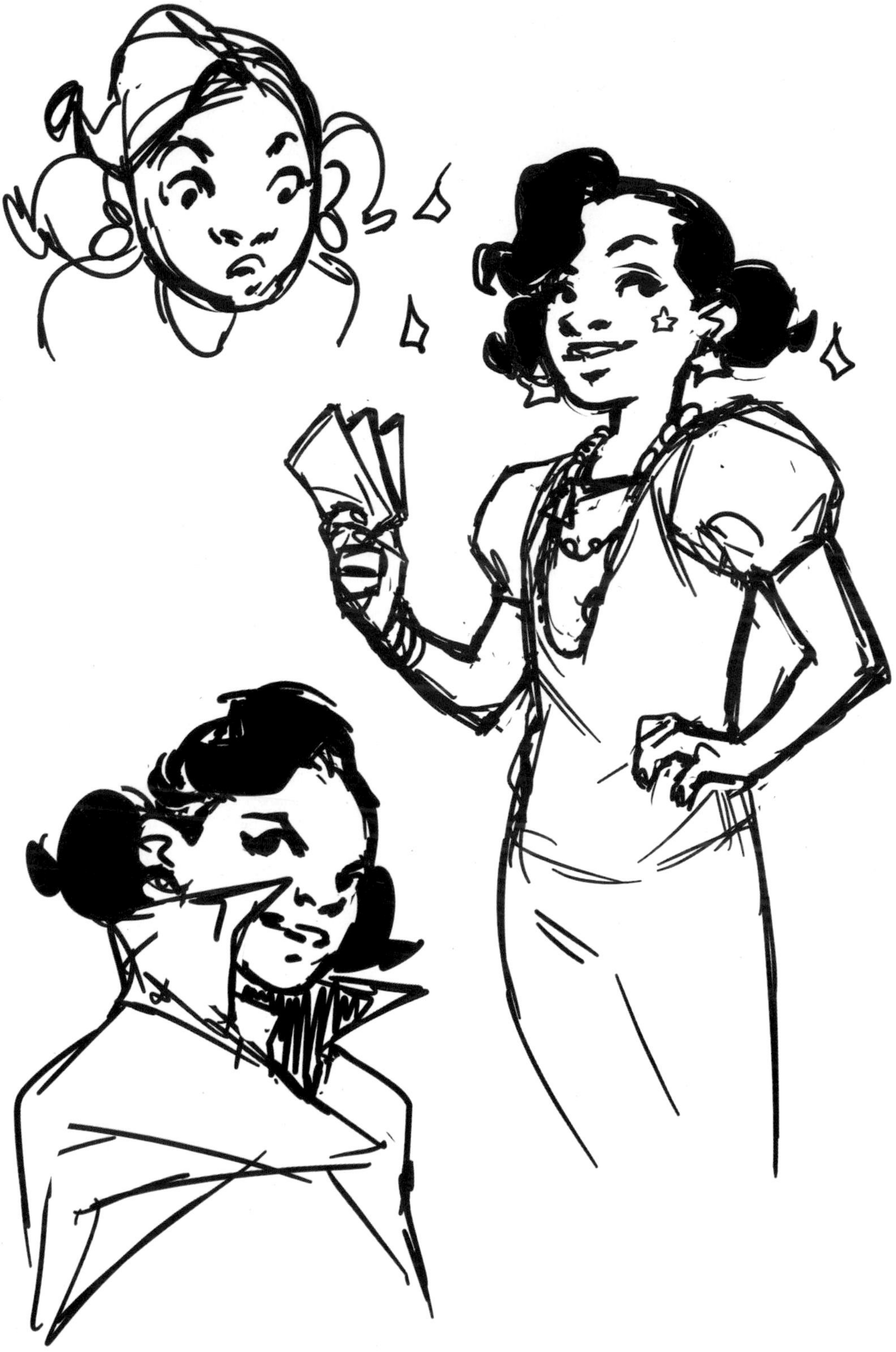

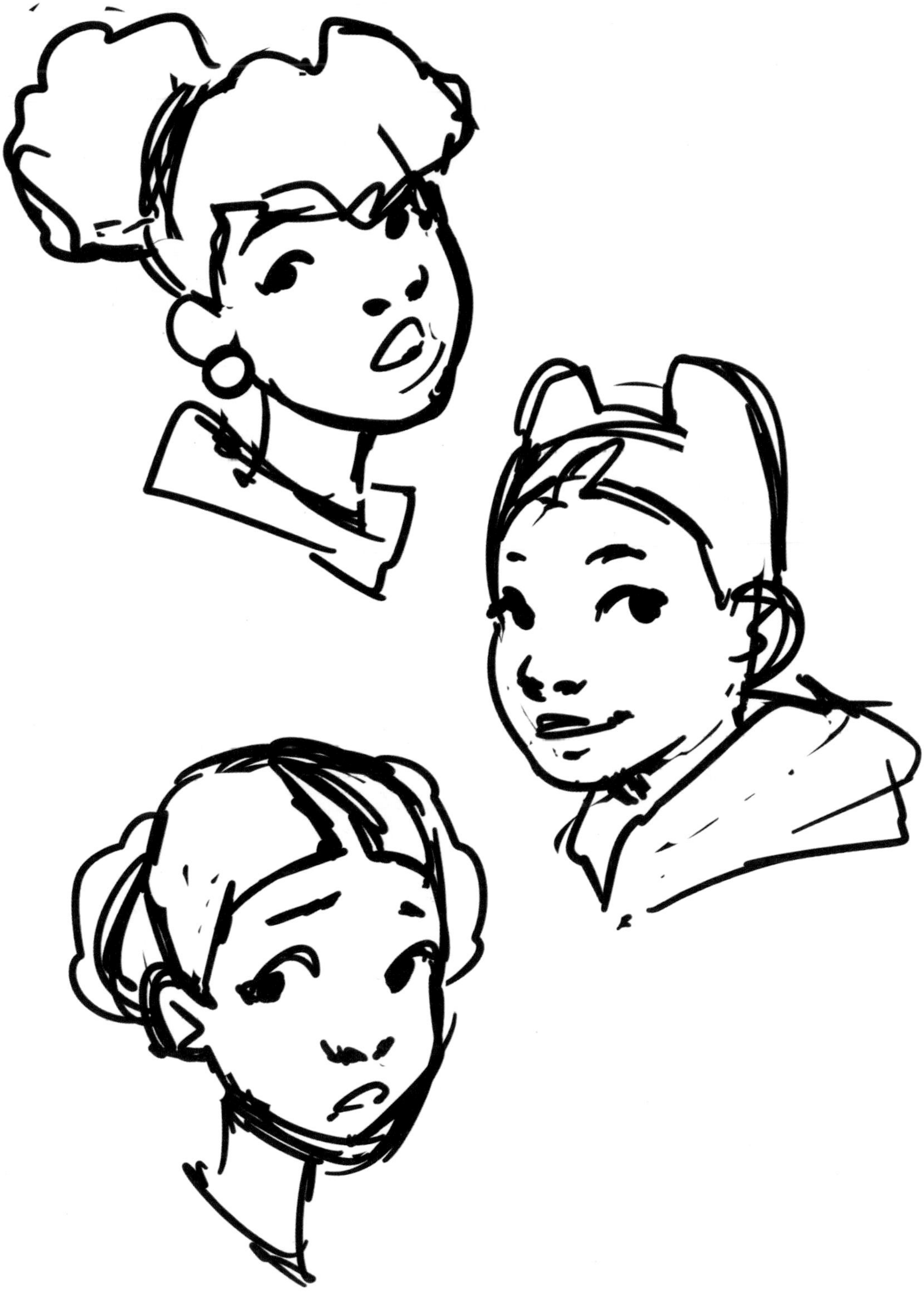

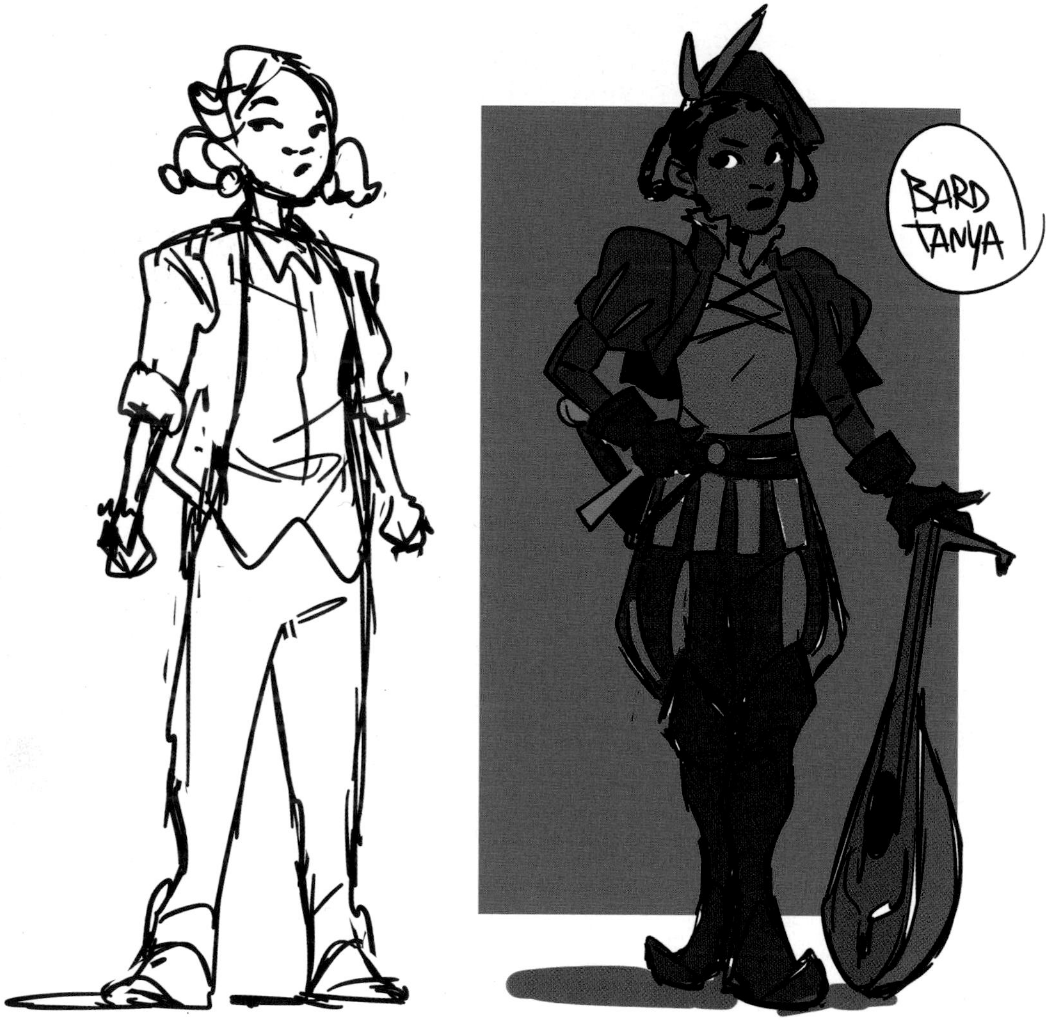
BARD TANYA

A LOVE THAT CROSSES LIGHT YEARS . . .

A sci-fi drama of a high school aged girl who belongs in a different time, a boy possessed by emptiness as deep as space, an alien artifact, mysterious murder, and a love that crosses light years . . .

When Amy's entire family is forced to move to Earth, Amy says goodbye to her best friend Jemmah and climbs into a cryotube to spend the next thirty years frozen in suspended animation, heading toward her new home. Her life will never by the same . . . and Jemmah is going to grow up without her. Once on Earth, Amy discovers high school only seemed difficult at first and a close group of friends has made the transition easier for Amy, but now she finds herself falling down a rabbit hole in her relationship with the mysterious, flavorless Oliver.

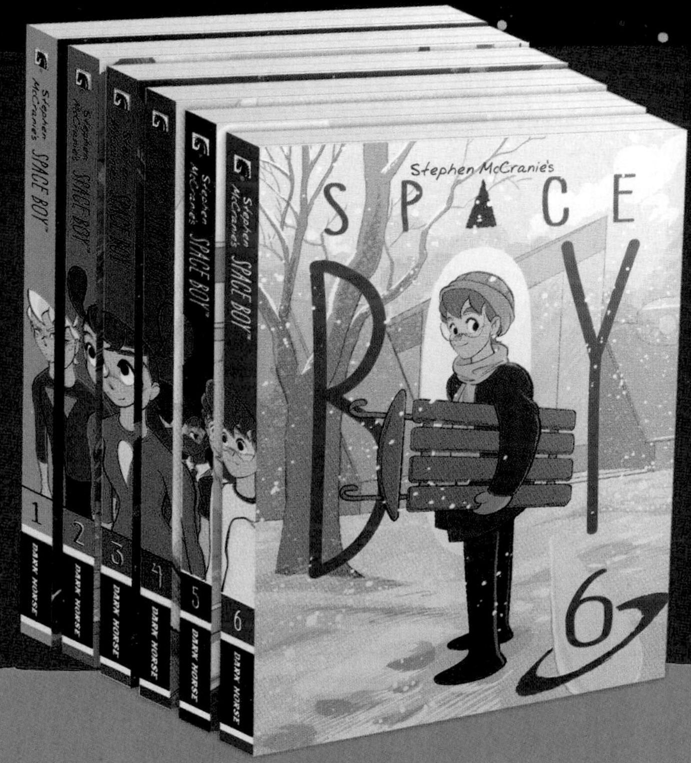
Stephen McCranie's
SPACE BOY
6
DARK HORSE

"TRULY ONE OF THE MOST THOUGHTFUL EXAMPLES I'VE EVER SEEN OF A TEENAGED GIRL IN FICTION."

–NARRATIVE INVESTIGATIONS

VOLUME 1
$10.99 • ISBN 978-1-50670-648-1

VOLUME 2
$10.99 • ISBN 978-1-50670-680-1

VOLUME 3
$10.99 • ISBN 978-1-50670-842-3

VOLUME 4
$10.99 • ISBN 978-1-50670-843-0

VOLUME 5
$10.99 • ISBN 978-1-50671-399-1

VOLUME 6
$10.99 • ISBN 978-1-50671-400-4

DARK HORSE BOOKS

AVAILABLE AT YOUR LOCAL COMICS SHOP OR BOOKSTORE!
TO FIND A COMICS SHOP IN YOUR AREA, VISIT COMICSHOPLOCATOR.COM
For more information or to order direct, visit darkhorse.com